FLAT STANLEY

4 Books in 1!

DON'T MISS THESE OTHER FLAT STANLEY STORIES:

Invisible Stanley

Stanley's Christmas Adventure

AND CATCH FLAT STANLEY'S WORLDWIDE ADVENTURES:

The Mount Rushmore Calamity

The Great Egyptian Grave Robbery

The Japanese Ninja Surprise

The Intrepid Canadian Expedition

The Amazing Mexican Secret

The African Safari Discovery

The Flying Chinese Wonders

The Australian Boomerang Bonanza

The US Capital Commotion

Showdown at the Alamo

Framed in France

Escape to California

FLAT STANLEY

4 Books in 1!

by Jeff Brown
Pictures by Macky Pamintuan

HARPER
An Imprint of HarperCollins*Publishers*

ISBN 978-0-06-249670-6

Typography by Jennifer Heuer
        18   19   20   PC/LSCH   10   9   8   7   6   5   4   3
❖
First Edition

FLAT STANLEY

CONTENTS

FLAT STANLEY

His Original Adventure!

For J.C. and Tony
—J.B.

CONTENTS

The Big Bulletin Board

Breakfast was ready.

"I will go wake the boys," Mrs. Lambchop said to her husband, George Lambchop. Just then their younger son, Arthur, called from the bedroom he shared with his brother, Stanley.

"Hey! Come and look! Hey!"

Mr. and Mrs. Lambchop were both

very much in favor of politeness and careful speech. "Hay is for horses, Arthur, not people," Mr. Lambchop said as they entered the bedroom. "Try to remember that."

"Excuse me," Arthur said. "But look!"

He pointed to Stanley's bed. Across it lay the enormous bulletin board that Mr. Lambchop had given the boys a Christmas ago so that they could pin up pictures and messages and maps. It had fallen, during the night, on top of Stanley.

But Stanley was not hurt. In fact, he would still have been sleeping if he had not been woken by his brother's shout.

"What's going on here?" he called out cheerfully from beneath the enormous board.

Mr. and Mrs. Lambchop hurried to lift it from the bed.

"Heavens!" said Mrs. Lambchop.

"Gosh!" said Arthur. "Stanley's flat!"

"As a pancake," said Mr. Lambchop. "Darndest thing I've ever seen."

"Let's all have breakfast," Mrs. Lambchop said. "Then Stanley and I will go see Dr. Dan and hear what he has to say."

In his office, Dr. Dan examined Stanley all over.

"How do you feel?" he asked. "Does it hurt very much?"

"I felt sort of tickly for a while after I got up," Stanley Lambchop said, "but I feel fine now."

"Well, that's mostly how it is with these cases," said Dr. Dan.

"We'll just have to keep an eye on

this young fellow," he said when he had finished the examination. "Sometimes we doctors, despite all our years of training and experience, can only marvel at how little we really know."

Mrs. Lambchop said she thought Stanley's clothes would have to be altered by the tailor now, so Dr. Dan told his nurse to take Stanley's measurements.

Mrs. Lambchop wrote them down.

Stanley was four feet tall, about a foot wide, and half an inch thick.

Being Flat

When Stanley got used to being flat, he enjoyed it. He could go in and out of rooms, even when the door was closed, just by lying down and sliding through the crack at the bottom.

Mr. and Mrs. Lambchop said it was silly, but they were quite proud of him.

Arthur got jealous and tried to slide

under a door, but he just banged his head.

Being flat could also be helpful, Stanley found.

He was taking a walk with Mrs. Lambchop one afternoon when her favorite ring fell from her finger. The ring rolled across the sidewalk and down between the bars of a grating that covered a deep, dark shaft. Mrs. Lambchop began to cry.

"I have an idea," Stanley said.

He took the laces out of his shoes and an extra pair out of his pocket and tied them all together to make one long lace. Then he tied one end of that to the back of his belt and gave the other end to his mother.

"Lower me," he said, "and I will look for the ring."

"Thank you, Stanley," Mrs. Lamb-chop said. She lowered him between the bars and moved him carefully up and down and from side to side, so that he could search the whole floor of the shaft.

Two policemen came by and stared at Mrs. Lambchop as she stood holding the long lace that ran down through the grating. She pretended not to notice them.

"What's the matter, lady?" the first policeman asked. "Is your yo-yo stuck?"

"I am not playing with a yo-yo!" Mrs. Lambchop said sharply. "My son is at the other end of this lace, if you must know."

"Get the net, Harry," said the second policeman. "We have caught a cuckoo!"

Just then, down in the shaft, Stanley cried out, "Hooray!"

Mrs. Lambchop pulled him up and saw that he had the ring.

"Good for you, Stanley," she said. Then she turned angrily to the policemen.

"A cuckoo, indeed!" she said. "Shame!"

The policemen apologized. "We didn't get it, lady," they said. "We have been hasty. We see that now."

"People should think twice before making rude remarks," said Mrs. Lambchop. "And then not make them at all."

The policemen realized that was a good rule and said they would try to remember it.

One day Stanley got a letter from his friend Thomas Anthony Jeffrey, whose family had moved recently to California. A school vacation was about to begin, and Stanley was invited to spend it with the Jeffreys.

"Oh, boy!" Stanley said. "I would love to go!"

Mr. Lambchop sighed. "A round-trip train or airplane ticket to California is very expensive," he said. "I will have to think of some cheaper way."

When Mr. Lambchop came home

from the office that evening, he brought with him an enormous brown-paper envelope.

"Now then, Stanley," he said. "Try this for size."

The envelope fit Stanley very well. There was even room left over, Mrs. Lambchop discovered, for an egg-salad sandwich made with thin bread, and a toothbrush case filled with milk.

They had to put a great many stamps on the envelope to pay for both airmail and insurance, but it was still much less expensive than a train or airplane ticket to California.

The next day Mr. and Mrs. Lambchop slid Stanley into his envelope, along with the egg-salad sandwich and the toothbrush case full of milk, and mailed him from the box on the corner. The

envelope had to be folded to fit through the slot, but Stanley was a limber boy, and inside the box he straightened right up again.

Mrs. Lambchop was nervous because Stanley had never been away from home alone before. She rapped on the box.

"Can you hear me, dear?" she called. "Are you all right?"

Stanley's voice came quite clearly. "I'm fine. Can I eat my sandwich now?"

"Wait an hour. And try not to get overheated, dear," Mrs. Lambchop said. Then she and Mr. Lambchop cried out, "Good-bye, good-bye!" and went home.

Stanley had a fine time in California.

When the visit was over, the Jeffreys returned him in a beautiful white envelope they had made themselves. It had red-and-blue markings to show that it was airmail, and Thomas Jeffrey had lettered it "Valuable" and "Fragile" and "This End Up" on both sides.

Back home Stanley told his family that he had been handled so carefully he never felt a single bump. Mr. Lambchop said it proved that jet planes were wonderful, and so was the Postal Service, and that this was a great age in which to live.

Stanley thought so too.

Stanley the Kite

Mr. Lambchop had always liked to take the boys out with him on Sunday afternoons, to a museum or roller-skating in the park, but it was difficult when they were crossing streets or moving about in crowds. Stanley and Arthur would often be jostled from his side and Mr. Lambchop worried about

speeding taxis or that hurrying people might accidentally knock them down.

It was easier after Stanley got flat.

Mr. Lambchop discovered that he could roll Stanley up without hurting him at all. He would tie a piece of string around Stanley to keep him from unrolling and make a little loop in the string for himself. It was as simple as carrying a parcel, and he could hold on to Arthur with the other hand.

Stanley did not mind being carried because he had never much liked to walk. Arthur didn't like to walk either, but he had to. It made him mad.

One Sunday afternoon, in the street, they met Ralph Jones, an old college friend of Mr. Lambchop's.

"Well, George, I see you have bought some wallpaper," Mr. Jones said. "Going to decorate your house, I suppose?"

"Wallpaper?" said Mr. Lambchop. "Oh, no. This is my son Stanley."

He undid the string and Stanley unrolled.

"How do you do?" Stanley said.

"Nice to meet you, young feller," the man said. "George," he said to Mr. Lambchop, "that boy is flat."

"Smart, too," Mr. Lambchop said. "Stanley is third from the top in his class at school."

"Phooey!" said Arthur.

"This is my younger son, Arthur," Mr. Lambchop said. "And

he will apologize for his rudeness."

Arthur could only blush and apologize.

Mr. Lambchop rolled Stanley up again and they set out for home. It rained quite hard while they were on the way. Stanley, of course, hardly got wet at all, just around the edges, but Arthur got soaked.

Late that night Mr. and Mrs. Lambchop heard a noise out in the living room. They found Arthur lying on the floor near the bookcase. He had piled a great many volumes of the *Encyclopaedia Britannica* on top of himself.

"Put some more on me," Arthur said

when he saw them. "Don't just stand there. Help me."

Mr. and Mrs. Lambchop sent him back to bed, but the next morning they spoke to Stanley. "Arthur can't help being jealous," they said. "Be nice to him. You're his big brother, after all."

The next Sunday, Stanley and Arthur went to the park by themselves. The day was sunny, but windy too, and many older boys were flying beautiful, enormous kites with long tails, made in all the colors of the rainbow.

Arthur sighed. "Someday," he said, "I will have a big kite, and I will win a kite-flying contest and be famous like everyone else. *Nobody* knows who I am these days."

Stanley remembered what his parents had said. He went to a boy whose kite was broken and borrowed a large spool of string.

"You can fly me, Arthur," he said. "Come on."

He attached the string to himself and gave Arthur the spool to hold. He ran lightly across the grass, sideways to get up speed, and then he turned to meet the breeze.

Up, up, up . . . UP! went Stanley, being a kite.

He knew just how to manage on the
gusts of wind. He faced full into the
wind if he wanted to rise, and let it
take him from behind when he wanted
speed. He had only to turn his thin
edge to the wind, carefully, a little at
a time, so that it did not hold him, and

then he would slip gracefully down toward the earth again.

Arthur let out all the string, and Stanley soared high above the trees, a beautiful sight in his red shirt and blue trousers against the pale blue sky.

Everyone in the park stood still to watch.

Stanley swooped right and then left in long, matched swoops. He held his arms by his sides and zoomed at the ground like a rocket and curved up again toward the sun. He side-slipped and circled, and made figure eights and crosses and a star.

Nobody has ever flown the way

Stanley Lambchop flew that day. Probably no one ever will again.

After a while, of course, people grew tired of watching, and Arthur got tired of running about with the empty spool. Stanley went right on, though, showing off.

Three boys came up to Arthur and invited him to join them for a hot dog and some soda pop. Arthur left the spool wedged in the fork of a tree. He did not notice, while he was eating the hot dog, that the wind was blowing the string and

tangling it about the tree.

The string got shorter and shorter, but Stanley did not realize how low he was until leaves brushed his feet, and then it was too late. He got stuck in the branches. Fifteen minutes passed before Arthur and the other boys heard his cries and climbed up to set him free.

Stanley would not speak to his brother that evening, and at bedtime, even though Arthur had apologized, he was still cross.

Alone with Mr. Lambchop in the living room, Mrs. Lambchop sighed and shook her head. "You're at the office all day, having fun," she said. "You don't realize what I go through with the boys. They're very difficult."

"Kids are like that," Mr. Lambchop said. "Phases. Be patient, dear."

The Museum Thieves

Mr. and Mrs. O. Jay Dart lived in the apartment above the Lambchops. Mr. Dart was an important man, the director of the Famous Museum of Art downtown in the city.

Stanley Lambchop had noticed in the elevator that Mr. Dart, who was ordinarily a cheerful man, had become quite gloomy, but he had no idea what

the reason was. And then at breakfast one morning he heard Mr. and Mrs. Lambchop talking about Mr. Dart.

"I see," said Mr. Lambchop, reading the paper over his coffee cup, "that still another painting has been stolen from the Famous Museum. It says here that Mr. O. Jay Dart, the director, is at his wits' end."

"Oh, dear! Are the police no help?" Mrs. Lambchop asked.

"It seems not," said Mr. Lambchop. "Listen to what the Chief of Police told the newspaper. 'We suspect a gang of sneak thieves. These are the worst kind. They work by sneakery, which makes them very difficult to catch. However,

THE DAILY SENTINEL
ANOTHER PAINTIN
STOLEN!

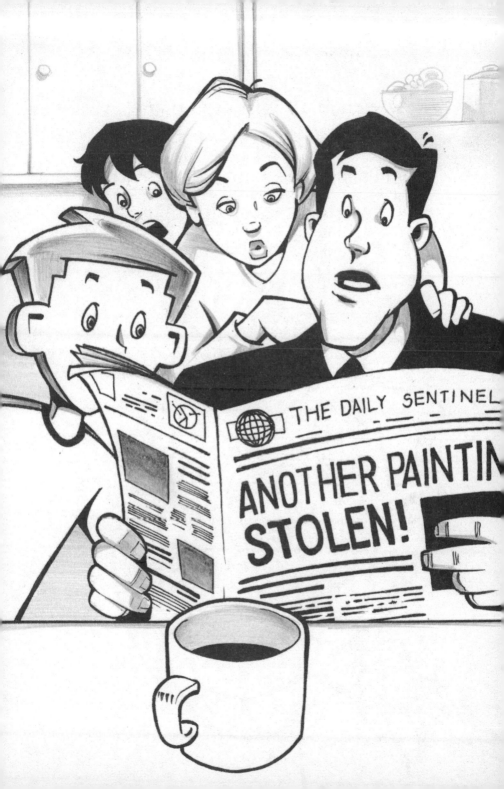

my men and I will keep trying. Meanwhile, I hope people will buy tickets for the Policemen's Ball and not park their cars where signs say don't.'"

The next morning
Stanley Lambchop heard
Mr. Dart talking to his
wife in the elevator.

"These sneak thieves work
at night," Mr. Dart said. "It
is very hard for our guards to
stay awake when they have been
on duty all day. And the Famous
Museum is so big, we cannot guard
every picture at the same time. I fear
it is hopeless, hopeless, hopeless!"

Suddenly, as if an electric light
bulb had lit up in the air above his
head, giving out little shooting lines
of excitement, Stanley Lambchop had
an idea. He told it to Mr. Dart.

"Stanley," Mr. Dart said, "if your mother will give her permission, I will put you and your plan to work this very night!"

Mrs. Lambchop gave her permission. "But you will have to take a long nap this afternoon," she said. "I won't have you up till all hours unless you do."

That evening, after a long nap, Stanley went with Mr. Dart to the Famous Museum. Mr. Dart took him into the main hall, where the biggest and most important paintings were hung. He pointed to a huge painting that showed a bearded man, wearing a floppy velvet hat, playing a violin for a lady who lay on a couch. There was

a half-man, half-horse person standing behind them, and three fat children with wings were flying around above. That, Mr. Dart explained, was the most expensive painting in the world!

There was an empty picture frame on the opposite wall. We shall hear more about that later on.

Mr. Dart took Stanley into his office and said, "It is time for you to put on a disguise."

"I already thought of that," Stanley Lambchop said, "and I brought one. My cowboy suit. It has a red bandanna that I can tie over my face. Nobody will recognize me in a million years."

"No," Mr. Dart said. "You will have

to wear the disguise I have chosen."

From a closet he took a white dress with a blue sash, a pair of shiny little pointed shoes, a wide straw hat with a blue band that matched the sash, and a wig and a stick. The wig was made of blond hair, long and done in ringlets. The stick was curved at the top and it, too, had a blue ribbon on it.

"In this shepherdess disguise," Mr. Dart said, "you will look like a painting that belongs in the main hall. We do not have cowboy pictures in the main hall."

Stanley was so disgusted, he could hardly speak. "I will look like a girl, that's what I will look like," he said. "I

wish I had never had my idea."

But he was a good sport, so he put on the disguise.

Back in the main hall, Mr. Dart helped Stanley climb up into the empty picture frame. Stanley was able to stay in place because Mr. Dart had cleverly put four small spikes in the wall, one for each hand and foot.

The frame was a perfect fit. Against the wall, Stanley looked just like a picture.

"Except for one thing," Mr. Dart said. "Shepherdesses are supposed to look happy. They smile at their sheep and at the sky. You look fierce, not happy, Stanley."

Stanley tried hard to get a faraway look in his eyes and even to smile a little bit.

Mr. Dart stood back a few feet and stared at him for a moment. "Well," he said, "it may not be art, but I know what I like."

He went off to make sure that certain other parts of Stanley's plan were taken care of, and Stanley was left alone.

It was very dark in the main hall. A little bit of moonlight came through the windows, and Stanley could just make out the world's most expensive painting on the opposite wall. He felt as though the bearded man with the violin and the lady on the couch and the half-horse person and the winged children were all waiting, as he was, for something to happen.

Time passed and he got tireder and tireder. Anyone would be tired this late at night, especially if he had to stand in a picture frame balancing on little spikes.

Maybe they won't come, Stanley thought. Maybe the sneak thieves won't come at all.

The moon went behind a cloud and then the main hall was pitch-dark. It seemed to get quieter, too, with the darkness. There was absolutely no sound at all. Stanley felt the hair on the back of his neck prickle beneath the golden curls of the wig.

Cr-eee-eee-k...

The creaking sound came from right out in the middle of the main hall, and even as he heard it, Stanley saw, in the same place, a tiny yellow glow of light!

The creaking came again, and the glow got bigger. A trapdoor had opened in the floor, and two men came up through it into the hall!

Stanley understood everything all at once. These must be the sneak thieves! They had a secret trapdoor entrance into the museum from outside. That was why they had never been caught. And now, tonight, they

were back to steal the most expensive painting in the world!

He held very still in his picture frame and listened to the sneak thieves.

"This is it, Max," said the first one. "This is where we art robbers pull a sensational job whilst the civilized community sleeps."

"Right, Luther," said the other man. "In all this great city, there is no one to suspect us."

Ha, ha! thought Stanley Lambchop. That's what you think!

The sneak thieves put down their lantern and took the world's most expensive painting off the wall.

"What would we do to anyone who tried to capture us, Max?" the first man asked.

"We would kill him. What else?" his friend replied.

That was enough to frighten Stanley, and he was even more frightened when

Luther came over and stared at him.

"This sheep girl," Luther said. "I thought sheep girls were supposed to smile, Max. This one looks scared."

Just in time, Stanley managed to get a faraway look in his eyes again and to smile, sort of.

"You're crazy, Luther," Max said. "She's smiling. And what a pretty little thing she is, too."

That made Stanley furious. He waited until the sneak thieves had turned back to the world's most expensive painting, and he shouted in his loudest, most terrifying voice: "POLICE! POLICE! MR. DART! THE SNEAK THIEVES ARE HERE!"

The sneak thieves looked at each other. "Max," said the first one, very quietly. "I think I heard the sheep girl yell."

"I think I did too," said Max in a quivery voice. "Oh, boy! Yelling pictures. We both need a rest."

"You'll get a rest, all right!" shouted Mr. Dart, rushing in with the Chief of Police and lots of guards and policemen behind him. "You'll get *ar-rested*, that's what! Ha, ha, ha!"

The sneak thieves were too mixed up by Mr. Dart's joke and too frightened by the policemen to put up a fight.

Before they knew it, they had been

handcuffed and led away to jail.

The next morning in the office of the Chief of Police, Stanley Lambchop got a medal. The day after that his picture was in all the newspapers.

Arthur's Good Idea

For a while Stanley Lambchop was a famous name. Everywhere that Stanley went, people stared and pointed at him. He could hear them whisper, "Over there, Agnes, over there! That must be Stanley Lambchop, the one who caught the sneak thieves . . ." and things like that.

But after a few weeks the whispering

and the staring stopped. People had other things to think about. Stanley did not mind. Being famous had been fun, but enough was enough.

And then came a further change, and it was not a pleasant one. People began to laugh and make fun of him as he passed by. "Hello, Super-Skinny!" they would shout, and even ruder things, about the way he looked.

Stanley told his parents how he felt. "It's the other kids I mostly mind," he said. "They don't like me anymore because I'm different. Flat."

"Shame on them," Mrs. Lambchop said. "It is wrong to dislike people for their shapes. Or their religion, for that matter, or the color of their skin."

"I know," Stanley said. "Only maybe it's impossible for everybody to like *everybody*."

"Perhaps," said Mrs. Lambchop. "But they can try."

Later that night Arthur Lambchop was woken by the sound of crying. In the darkness he crept across the room and knelt by Stanley's bed.

"Are you okay?" he said.

"Go away," Stanley said.

"Don't be mad at me," Arthur said. "You're still mad because I let you get tangled the day you were my kite, I guess."

"Skip it, will you?" Stanley said.

"I'm not mad. Go away."

"Please let's be friends. . . ." Arthur couldn't help crying a little, too. "Oh, Stanley," he said. "Please tell me what's wrong."

Stanley waited for a long time before he spoke. "The thing is," he said, "I'm just not happy anymore. I'm tired of being flat. I want to be a regular shape again, like other people. But I'll have to go on being flat forever. It makes me sick."

"Oh, Stanley," Arthur said. He dried his tears on a corner of Stanley's sheet and could think of nothing more to say.

"Don't talk about what I just said," Stanley told him. "I don't want the

folks to worry. That would only make it worse."

"You're brave," Arthur said. "You really are."

He took hold of Stanley's hand. The two brothers sat together in the darkness, being friends. They were both still sad, but each one felt a *little* better than he had before.

And then, suddenly, though he was not even trying to think, Arthur had an idea. He jumped up and turned on the light and ran to the big storage box where toys and things were kept. He began to rummage in the box.

Stanley sat up in bed to watch.

Arthur flung aside a football and

some lead soldiers and airplane models and lots of wooden blocks, and then he said, "Aha!" He had found what he wanted—an old bicycle pump. He held it up, and Stanley and he looked at each other.

"Okay," Stanley said at last. "But take it easy." He put the end of the long pump hose in his mouth and clamped his lips tightly about it so that no air could escape.

"I'll go slowly," Arthur said. "If it hurts or anything, wiggle your hand at me."

He began to pump. At first nothing happened except that Stanley's cheeks bulged a bit. Arthur watched his hand,

but there was no wiggle signal, so he pumped on. Then, suddenly, Stanley's top half began to swell.

"It's working! It's working!" shouted Arthur, pumping away.

Stanley spread his arms so that the air could get around inside him more easily. He got bigger and bigger. The buttons of his pajama top burst off—*Pop! Pop! Pop!* A moment more and he was all rounded out; head and body, arms and legs. But not his right foot. That foot stayed flat.

Arthur stopped pumping. "It's like trying to do the very last bit of those long balloons," he said. "Maybe a shake would help."

Stanley shook his right foot twice, and with a little *whooshing* sound it swelled out to match the left one. There stood Stanley Lambchop as he used to be, as if he had never been flat at all.

"Thank you, Arthur," Stanley said. "Thank you very much."

The brothers were shaking hands when Mr. Lambchop strode into the room with Mrs. Lambchop right behind him. "We heard you!" said Mr. Lambchop. "Up and talking when you ought to be asleep, eh? Shame on—"

"GEORGE!" said Mrs. Lambchop. "Stanley's *round* again!"

"You're right!" said Mr. Lambchop, noticing. "Good for you, Stanley!"

"I'm the one who did it," Arthur said. "I blew him up."

Everyone was terribly excited and happy, of course. Mrs. Lambchop made hot chocolate to celebrate the occasion, and several toasts were drunk to Arthur for his cleverness.

When the little party was over, Mr. and Mrs. Lambchop tucked the boys back into their beds and kissed them, and then they turned out the light. "Good night," they said.

"Good night," said Stanley and Arthur.

It had been a long and tiring day. Very soon all the Lambchops were asleep.

The End

FLAT STANLEY

Stanley, Flat Again!

For Peter and Wendy,
Ozinger, Betsy, and Ash

CONTENTS

SPORTS

CHAMPS!

34

A Morning Surprise

Mrs. Lambchop was making breakfast. Mr. Lambchop, at the kitchen table, helped by reading bits from the morning paper.

"Here's an odd one, Harriet," he said. "There's a chicken in Sweden that rides a bike."

"So do I, George," said Mrs. Lambchop, not really listening.

"Listen to this. 'Merker Building emptied. To be collapsed next week.' Imagine! Eight floors!"

"Poor thing!" Mrs. Lambchop set out plates. "Boys!" she called. "Breakfast is ready!"

Her glance fell upon a row of photographs on the wall above the sink. There was a smiling Stanley, only half an inch thick, his big bulletin board having fallen from the bedroom wall to rest upon him overnight. Next came reminders of the many family adventures that had come after Stanley's younger brother, Arthur, had cleverly blown him round again with a bicycle pump. There were the brothers with

Prince Haraz, the young genie who had granted wishes for them all after being accidentally summoned by Stanley from a lamp. There was the entire family with Santa Claus and his daughter, Sarah, taken during a Christmas visit to the North Pole. There was the family again in Washington, D.C., in the office of the President of the United States, who had asked them to undertake a secret mission into outer space. The last picture showed Arthur standing beside a balloon on which Mrs. Lambchop had painted a picture of Stanley's face. The balloon, its string in fact held by Stanley, had been a valuable guide to his presence, since he was invisible at the time. "Boys!" she called again. "Breakfast!"

In their bedroom, Stanley and Arthur had finished dressing.

While Stanley filled his backpack, Arthur bounced a tennis ball. "Let's go," he said. "Here! Catch!"

Stanley had just reached for a book on the shelf by his bed. The ball struck his back as he turned, and he banged his shoulder on a corner of the shelf.

"Ouch!"

"Sorry," Arthur said. "But let's go, okay? You know how long— STANLEY!"

"Why are you shouting?" Stanley adjusted his pack. "C'mon! I'm so hungry—" He paused. "Oh, boy!

Arthur, do you see?"

"I do, actually." Arthur swallowed hard. "You're, you know . . . flat."

The brothers stared at each other.

"The pump?" Stanley said. "It might work again."

Arthur fetched the bicycle pump from their toy chest, and Stanley lay on his bed with the hose end in his mouth.

Arthur gave a long, steady, pump.

Stanley made a face. "That hurts!"

Arthur pumped again, and Stanley snatched the hose from his mouth. "Owww! That really hurts! It wasn't like that before. We'd better stop."

"Now what?" Arthur said. "We can't just hide in here forever, you know."

Mrs. Lambchop's call came again. "Boys! Please come!"

"Do me a favor," Stanley said. "You tell them. Sort of get them ready, okay?"

"Okay," said Arthur, and went to tell.

Arthur stood in the kitchen doorway. "Hey, guess what?" he said.

"Hay is for horses, dear," said Mrs. Lambchop. "Good morning! Breakfast is ready."

"Good morning, Arthur," Mr. Lambchop said from behind his newspaper. "Where's Stanley?"

"Guess what?" Arthur said again.

Mrs. Lambchop sighed. "Oh, all right! I can't guess. Tell."

"Stanley's flat again," said Arthur.

Mr. Lambchop put down his paper.

Mrs. Lambchop closed her eyes. "Flat again? Is that what you said?"

"Yes," said Arthur.

"It's true." Stanley stood now beside Arthur in the doorway. "Just look."

"Good grief!" said Mr. Lambchop. "I can't believe that bulletin board—"

"It didn't fall on me this time," Stanley said. "I just got flat. Arthur tried to pump me up, like before, but it hurt too much."

"Oh, Stanley!" Mrs. Lambchop ran to kiss him. "How do you feel now?"

"Fine, actually," Stanley said. "Just surprised. Can I go to school?"

Mrs. Lambchop thought for a moment. "Very well. Eat your breakfast. After school we'll hear what Dr. Dan has to say."

Dr. Dan

"Ah, Mr. and Mrs. Lambchop! And the boys!" said Dr. Dan as they entered his office. "How nice to—"

His eyes widened. "Good heavens, Stanley! Mr. Lambchop, you really must do something about that bulletin board!"

"It is still firmly in place, Dr. Dan,"

Mrs. Lambchop said. "We are at a loss to account for this attack of flatness."

"Hmmm." Dr. Dan thought for a moment. "Is there, perhaps, a family history of flatness?"

"No," Mr. Lambchop said. "We'd remember that."

"We got dressed for school," Stanley explained. "We didn't even have breakfast. And all of a sudden, I got flat."

Dr. Dan frowned. "Nothing happened? Nothing at all?"

"Well, Arthur hit me with a tennis ball," Stanley said. "And then I banged my shoulder on—"

"Aha!" Jumping up, Dr. Dan took a large book from the case behind his desk and began turning pages. "This is Dr. Franz Gemeister's excellent *Difficult and Peculiar Cases.* Just let me find . . . here it is! 'Flatness, page two seventeen!'"

He read aloud. "'Sudden flatness . . . extremely rare . . . minimal documentation . . . hearsay reports . . .' Ah, here it is! Dates back to the fifth century! 'During battle, Mongo the Fierce, an

aide to Attila the Hun, was struck twice, simultaneously, from behind, and at once became no thicker than his shield. He became known as Mongo the Plate, and lived to old age without regaining his original girth.'"

Dr. Dan closed the book. "As I suspected! The OBP."

"Beg pardon?" said Mrs. Lambchop.

"The OBP. Osteal Balance Point," Dr. Dan explained. "A little-known anatomical feature. The human body, of course, is a complex miracle, its skeleton a delicate framework of supports and balances. The Osteal Balance Point may occur almost anywhere in the upper torso. It is vulnerable only to the application of simultaneous pressures at two points which vary depending on the age and particular 'design,' let us say, of the individual involved. In my opinion, the pressures created by the tennis ball and the shelf corner affected Stanley's OBP, thereby turning him flat."

For a moment, everyone was silent.

"The first time Stanley went flat, you were greatly puzzled by his condition," Mr. Lambchop said at last. "Now you seem remarkably well informed."

"I read up on it," said Dr. Dan.

Mrs. Lambchop sighed. "Perhaps we should seek a second opinion. Who is the world's leading authority on the OBP?"

"That would be me," said Dr. Dan.

"I see. . . . Well, we've taken enough of your time." Mr. Lambchop rose, motioning his family to follow. "Thank you, Dr. Dan."

At the door, Mrs. Lambchop turned. "Perhaps if we found the, you know, the OBP, we could make Stanley—"

"No, no!" said Dr. Dan. "It would be dangerous to put the lad through such a skeletal strain again! And finding the OBP? Not very likely, I'm afraid."

Arthur had an idea. "I know! If we all got sticks and hit Stanley all over at the same time, and kept doing it, then—"

"That will do, Arthur," Mr. Lambchop said, and led his family out.

Stanley Sails

Early the next Sunday morning, Mr. Lambchop had a call from an old college friend, Ralph Jones.

"Just wanted to remind you, George, that Stanley and I have a date to go sailing today," he said.

"He's looking forward to it, Ralph." Mr. Lambchop hesitated. "I should mention, perhaps, that Stanley has gone flat again."

Mr. Jones sighed. "I thought he'd got over that. Well, I'll pick him up at ten."

Later that morning, driving with Stanley to his sailing club on the seashore, Mr. Jones inquired about a foreign visitor he had once met with the Lambchops. "A prince, yes? He around these days?"

Stanley knew he meant the young genie, Prince Haraz, but it would be difficult to explain not only the genie part, but also that Haraz had returned to the genie kingdom from which he had come.

"No," Stanley said. "He went home, actually."

"Too bad." Mr. Jones was famous for

his amazing memory. "Haraz, as I recall. Prince Fawzi Mustafa Aslan Mirza Malek Namerd Haraz?"

"Right," said Stanley.

In the harbor of the sailing club, Mr. Jones prepared his boat, *Lovebug*, and explained it to Stanley. "This big sail here is the mainsail, and that's the rudder back there, for steering. In this zip bag is another sail, called a spinnaker. We'll use that one for extra speed when we're running before the wind. See that boat way out there, how its spinnaker is puffing out front?"

Stanley laughed. The spinnaker looked like an open umbrella lying on its side.

"See over there," Mr. Jones went on, "between the committee boat, with the judges on it, and the red buoy? That's the starting line. The race ends back there too. First boat to cross that line wins!"

He cast off the mooring line, and the mainsail filled. *Lovebug* headed out to join the other boats.

Mr. Jones pointed. "There! That's Jasper Green's boat, *Windswept*. He's the one I want especially to beat!"

"Why? Are you mad at him?" Stanley asked.

"He was very rude to me once. But never mind. Let's just make sure we win!"

Behind the start line, they found

themselves beside *Windswept*. Jasper Green gave a friendly wave, but Ralph Jones ignored him.

"You're always in a bad mood with me, Ralph," Mr. Green said. "Why? I don't— Here we go!"

A pistol shot had signaled the start of the race. *Lovebug* and *Windswept* and the other racers glided across the start line behind the motor-powered committee boat, which led them along a course marked by buoys with bright green streamers.

Stanley sat back, enjoying himself. The sun was bright, the breeze fresh against his face, the sky clear and blue, the water a beautiful slate color. There

were boats on both sides of them, boats ahead, boats behind. How pretty they were, their white sails making cheerful crackling sounds as they billowed in the wind!

Along the shore, people waved from the porches of houses, their voices carrying faintly on the wind. "Way to go! ... Looking good, sailors! ... Looking flat, one of them!" Stanley waved back, knowing that the teasing was kindly meant.

Lovebug passed other boats, but there were many more still ahead. And now they were almost abreast of *Windswept.*

Stanley saw that Jasper Green had hoisted his spinnaker, and that other boats had too.

"I've got you beat, Ralph!" Jasper Green shouted.

"We'll just round this point, Stanley! Then— Now!" exclaimed Ralph Jones. "Let's show Jasper what running before the wind really means!"

He attached his spinnaker to a halyard and ran it up the mast. *Who-o-oosh!* The spinnaker billowed out, and Stanley felt *Lovebug* surge forward, as if pushed by an invisible hand.

"Here we go!" shouted Ralph Jones.

They passed five more boats, three more, then *Windswept*! They were ahead of everyone now, and the finish line lay ahead!

"We're going to win!" Stanley shouted.

"Yes!" Ralph Jones shouted back. "Just wait till Jasper—"

R-i-i-i-i-p!

The sound came from above. Looking up, they saw that the top of the spinnaker had torn.

R-i-i-i-i-i-i-i-p!

The rip streaked downward, and now the spinnaker, torn all the way down, flapped uselessly in the wind. *Lovebug* slowed.

"Drat!" Mr. Jones did his best with the mainsail. "Drat, drat, drat!"

Windswept came up behind them. "Tough luck!" called Jasper Green. "Ha, ha!"

"Drat!" Mr. Jones sighed. "Nothing we can do, Stanley. Unless— This may be crazy, but . . . Stanley, perhaps you could be our spinnaker?"

"What?" Stanley shouted. "How?"

"Good question," said Mr. Jones. "Let's see. . . . First, go take hold of the mast. That's it. Now maybe—"

"Excuse me," Stanley said. "But did you ever do this before?"

"Stanley, *nobody* ever did this before." Mr. Jones took a deep breath. "Okay. Now twist around to face forward, and grab the mast behind you above your head!"

Stanley did as he was told, planting his feet on the sides of the boat to hold him in place. The wind pressed him from behind, driving *Lovebug* toward the finish line.

"Yes! Chest forward! Butt back!" shouted Mr. Jones. "Best spinnaker I ever had!" In a moment they had passed *Windswept*, and Stanley could not help laughing at the surprise on Jasper Green's face.

And then they were across the finish line! *Lovebug* had won!

Back in the clubhouse, Jasper Green would not admit that he had lost. A flat person used as a sail? He had never seen *that* before, he said, and went to the race committee office to complain. But he returned shortly to report that *Lovebug* had indeed won. The committee had advised him, he said, that there was no rule against a crew member allowing the wind to blow against him.

"Great sailing, Ralph!" he said. "I thought it was my race, I really did!"

"Thank you, Jasper," Mr. Jones said, but Stanley noticed that he did not smile.

Jasper Green noticed too. "Ralph, you're still mad at me," he said. "But *why*?"

"You spilled coffee on my white pants,

Jasper," said Ralph Jones. "And you just laughed when I jumped up."

"What?" Jasper Green seemed greatly surprised. "I don't remember— Where? When?"

"We were having lunch," said Mr. Jones. "At the old Vandercook Hotel."

"The Vandercook? It closed down twenty years ago!" Mr. Green slapped his forehead. "I *do* remember! That lunch was twenty years ago, Ralph!"

"Twenty-one, actually."

"All right, all right!" said Mr. Green. "I apologize, for heaven's sake!"

Ralph Jones smiled warmly. "Perfectly all right, Jasper," he said. "Don't give it another thought."

Back to School

Stanley was pleased that his classmates, who still remembered his previous flatness, made no great fuss about it now. Mostly they expressed only cheerful interest. "Feeling okay, Stan?" they said, and "Lookin' sharp, man! Sharp, see? Get the joke?" Only mean Emma Weeks was unpleasant. "Huh!

Mr. Show-off again!" Emma said one day, but Stanley pretended not to hear.

He had been back at school for a week when a newspaper, learning of this unusually shaped student, sent a photographer to investigate. He found Stanley watching a practice on the soccer field.

"Flash Tobin," he said. "From the *Daily Sentinel*. You're the flat kid, right?"

Stanley thought he must be joking. "How did you know?" he said, joking back.

"How did I—" The photographer laughed. "Oh, I get it! Can I take your picture, kid? Right here by the goal posts?"

Stanley nodded, and Flash Tobin took his picture. "I heard there was a flat kid here before," he said. "Helped catch sneak thieves at the Famous Museum of Art. But that kid, I heard he got round again."

"It was me," Stanley told him.

"You go back and forth, huh?"

The photographer was impressed. "Okay, get round now. I'd like a shot of that too."

"I can't just do it when I want," Stanley explained. "The first time, my brother had to blow me up. With a bicycle pump."

"Make a great picture!" Flash Tobin shook his head. "Well, we'll just go with flat."

Stanley's picture was in the *Daily Sentinel* the next morning, and Arthur could not help showing his jealousy. Stanley was always getting his picture in the paper, he said. Didn't they see how interesting it would be to have a picture of his brother?

There was a soccer team practice that afternoon, and the day was windy. It was worrisome, the coach said, the way Stanley got blown about. Perhaps, for the sake of the team, he should switch to an indoor sport.

Stanley loved soccer, and the more he thought about what the coach had said, the sadder he felt.

Miss Elliott, his homeroom teacher, noticed that he was not his usual cheerful self. "Mr. Redfield, the new guidance counselor, is said to be very helpful to troubled students," she told him. "I will ask him to find time for you."

Miss Elliott spoke to him again after lunch. "Such good luck, Stanley! Mr. Redfield will see you right after school today!"

"Come in, Stanley. Sit right there!" Mr. Redfield pointed to a comfortable chair.

Stanley sat, and Mr. Redfield leaned back behind his desk. "Now then. . . . You do understand that anything you say here is completely confidential? I won't tell anybody."

Stanley wondered what he could say that would interest anybody else.

"Miss Elliott tells me you seem troubled." Mr. Redfield lowered his voice. "What's wrong?"

"I'm not sure, actually," Stanley said.

Mr. Redfield picked up a pad and a pen. "Speak freely. Whatever comes into your head. Anything special happen lately?"

"Well, I got flat," Stanley said.

Mr. Redfield made a note on his pad. "I do see that, yes. How did that make you feel?"

Stanley thought for a moment. "Flat."

"I see." Mr. Redfield nodded. "This

flatness, it's come upon you before, I'm told. Is it possible that somehow, without even admitting it to yourself, you wanted it to happen again?"

"No way!" Stanley said firmly. "The first time, it was kind of fun for a while. Flying like a kite, and being mailed to California, things like that. But then I got, you know, tired of it. And now I might get put off the soccer team."

Mr. Redfield nodded again. "You take no pleasure now in your unusual shape?"

Stanley thought for a moment. "Well, sometimes." He told about being a sail, and helping Ralph Jones win a race.

Mr. Redfield made another note. "I

see. This dream of being a sail, have you dreamed it before?"

Stanley stared at him. "It wasn't a . . . it really happened! I'm just tired of being different, I guess."

Mr. Redfield pressed his fingertips together. "Different? How do you feel different, would you say?"

Stanley wondered how Mr. Redfield could be a good guidance counselor if he had both terrible eyesight and a terrible memory.

"Well, I'm the only one in my class who's flat," he said. "The whole school, actually."

"Interesting." Mr. Redfield made another note and glanced at his watch.

"I'm afraid our time is up, Stanley. Would you like to see me again? Just let Miss Elliott know."

"Okay," Stanley said politely, but he didn't think he would.

Why Me?

Stanley had looked sad all evening, Arthur thought. At bedtime, as they lay waiting for Mr. and Mrs. Lambchop to come say good night, he wondered how to cheer his brother up.

It was raining hard, and he remembered suddenly the rainy evening that Stanley had snacked on raisins, and by morning had become invisible. A little-known consequence, Dr. Dan had explained, of eating fruit during bad weather.

"Hear the rain, Stanley?" he said. "Better not eat any fruit."

"Ha, ha, ha." Stanley sounded cross. "Just leave me alone, okay?"

"Stanley's in a terrible mood," Arthur told Mr. and Mrs. Lambchop when they came in "He won't even talk to me."

"What's wrong, my boy?" Mr Lambchop asked.

"Nothing." Stanley put his pillow over his head.

"If my picture was in the newspaper practically every day, I'd be happy," Arthur said. "I mean, why—"

Mrs. Lambchop hushed him. "Stanley, dear? What is troubling you?"

"Nothing. Nothing," Stanley said from under the pillow, and sat up. "But why me? Why am I always getting flat, or invisible or something? Why can't it just once be someone else?"

"I wouldn't mind, actually," Arthur said. "Just for a while. I—"

"Hush, Arthur!" Mrs. Lambchop

put out the overhead light, lit a corner lamp, and sat by Stanley on his bed. Mr. Lambchop sat with Arthur. The gentle patter of the rain against the windows, the glow of the little lamp, made the bedroom cozy indeed.

"I do see what you mean, Stanley," Mr. Lambchop said at last. "Why do these things happen to you? Your mother and I don't know the answer either. But things often happen without there seeming to be a reason, and then something else happens, and suddenly the first thing seems to have had a purpose after all."

"Well put, George!" Mrs. Lambchop squeezed Stanley's hand. "What we do know, Stanley dear, is that we're very proud of you, and love you very much. And we understand about the flatness, and all the other unexpected happenings, how upsetting it must be."

"It sure is!" said Stanley. "How would you like never knowing when you might get flat? Or invisible? Maybe someday I'll wake up ten feet tall or one inch short, or with green hair, or a tail or something!"

"I know. . . ." Mrs. Lambchop said softly, and Mr. Lambchop came and patted Stanley's shoulder. Then they kissed both boys, switched off the lamp, and went out.

Arthur spoke into the darkened

room. "Stanley?"

"I'm trying to sleep," said Stanley. "What?"

"I was just thinking," Arthur said. "If you got invisible, and then you got flat, how would they know?"

"Huh? I don't—" Stanley laughed. "Oh, I get it! About the flatness. Good one, Arthur."

Arthur laughed too.

"Quiet, please," said Stanley. "I'm trying to sleep."

"Okay," Arthur said, but he chuckled several times before he fell asleep.

Emma

Mr. Lambchop came home early the next afternoon, full of excitement.

"Guess what?" he said. "The old Merker Department Store downtown? Eight floors, all emptied out, waiting to be torn down? Well, last night most of it fell down by itself!" He switched on the TV. "News time! Let's get the latest!"

". . . more on the Merker building collapse!" a newscaster was saying. "It's just a mountain of rubble now, folks! Three workmen have been treated for minor bruises, but no other injuries are reported. The public is requested to avoid the area until—"

A young woman ran on, handed him a slip of paper, and ran off again.

"Hold on! This just in!" The newscaster read from the slip. "Wow! A little girl is trapped under all that wreckage! Emma Weeks, daughter of local businessman Oswald Weeks!"

"Emma Weeks!" Stanley exclaimed. "She's in my class! No wonder she wasn't at school today!"

"Emma's not hurt, it appears," the newscaster continued. "Firemen called to the scene can hear her calling up through chinks in the wreckage, demanding food and water! But Fire Chief Johnson has forbidden any rescue efforts! Any disturbance, any shifting  of the wreckage, he says, might bring the rest of the building crashing down! Now, here's Tom Miller!"

The TV screen showed a reporter with a microphone standing by the wrecked building.

"Emma Weeks!"
shouted the reporter,
holding his microphone up to
a crack. "Do you hear me?
Are you all right?"

Emma's voice was faint

but clear. "Oh, sure! I'm just great! I hope a building falls on me every day, you know? C'mon, get me out of here!"

Mrs. Lambchop sighed. "Such an unfortunate tone! She is under great strain, of course."

"Emma's always like that," Stanley said.

Half an hour later, while Mrs. Lambchop was preparing supper, a siren sounded outside, then died away. Opening the front door, Mr. Lambchop saw a Fire Department car at the curb. On the doorstep stood Fire Chief Johnson and a very worried-looking man and woman.

"Mr. Lambchop?" said Chief Johnson.

"I'll get right to the point, sir. I reckon you heard about little Emma Weeks, trapped in the Merker wreck? Well, Mr. and Mrs. Weeks here, and me, we'd like a word with you folks."

"Of course!" Mr. Lambchop led the visitors into the house and introduced them to his family.

"Oh, Mrs. Weeks!" Mrs. Lambchop cried. "Your poor daughter! You must be dreadfully worried!"

"We are indeed!" said Mr. Weeks. "But Chief Johnson thinks your Stanley might be able to save Emma!"

"Who, me?" and "Who, Stanley?" said Stanley and Arthur.

Chief Johnson explained. "Problem is

that if a policeman, or one of my firemen, tries to dig his way in to Emma, the whole rest of the building could crash down on 'em! Too bad we don't have a flat fireman, I was thinking. Flat fella could squeeze through all those narrow openings we know are there, 'cause we hear Emma when she calls. Then

I recollected the newspaper story, with a picture of Stanley here. Hit me right away! *That* boy could maybe wiggle in to Emma!"

For a moment, everyone was silent. Then Mrs. Lambchop shook her head.

"It sounds terribly dangerous," she said. "I'm sorry, but I must say no."

"It is a tad risky, ma'am," said Chief Johnson. "But we've got to remember the boy is already flat."

Mrs. Weeks sobbed. "Oh, poor Emma! How are we to save her?"

Mrs. Lambchop bit her lip.

Stanley remembered something. "I was just thinking." He turned to Mr. Lambchop. "The other night? When I got mad about all the crazy things that keep happening to me? Remember what you said? You said that sometimes things happen that nobody can see a reason for, and then afterwards some other thing happens, and all of a sudden it seems like the first thing had a reason after all. Well, I was just thinking that me getting flat again was one crazy thing, and that maybe Emma getting stuck where I'm the only one who can try to save her, that might be the second thing."

Mr. Lambchop nodded, and took Mrs. Lambchop's hand. "We should be very proud of our son, Harriet."

Mrs. Lambchop thought for a

moment. "Stanley," she said at last. "Will you be very, very, careful not to let that enormous building fall on you?"

"Okay. Sure," Stanley said.

Mrs. Lambchop turned to Mr. and Mrs. Weeks. "We will allow Stanley to help," she said. "He will do his best for Emma."

"Fine boy we got here! Brave as a lion!" shouted Chief Johnson. "Now listen up, folks! Mrs. Lambchop, you help me get things ready! Then Stanley can go right in after Emma! Got that? Everybody meet us at the Merker Building, thirty minutes from now!"

Where Are You, Emma?

In the late afternoon sunlight, at the remains of the old Merker building, the Lambchops and the Weekses watched Chief Johnson prepare Stanley for his rescue attempt. Flash Tobin, the *Daily Sentinel* photographer, was there too, taking pictures.

Mrs. Lambchop had supplied two slices of bread and cheese, each wrapped in plastic, and her grandfather's flat silver cigarette case filled with grape soda. Chief Johnson taped the bread and cheese packets to Stanley's arms and legs, the cigarette case to his chest, and gave him a small, flat flashlight.

Then he led Stanley up to a tall crack in the wreckage. "Emma!" he shouted. "Fella's coming to help you! When he calls your name, you holler back 'Here!' so he knows which way to go. Got that?"

Emma's voice came faintly. "Yeah, yeah! Hurry up! I'm starving!"

Chief Johnson shook Stanley's hand. "Good luck, son!"

The evening sunlight glowed warmly

on the red bricks of the fallen building as Stanley stepped close to the crack. Mrs. Lambchop waved to him, and Stanley waved back. How handsome he is, she thought. How brave, how tall, how flat!

Stanley took two steps forward and disappeared sideways through the crack. A moment later they heard his shout. "Hey! It's really dark in here!"

"Hay is for horses, Stanley!" Mrs. Lambchop called back. "Oh, never mind! Good luck, dear!"

This was a dark greater than any he had ever known. Stanley could almost feel the blackness on his skin.

He clicked on his flashlight and edged forward without difficulty, but then the crack narrowed, slowing him. The bread slice on his left leg had scraped something, loosening the tape that held it. Pressing the tape back into place, he wiggled forward until he came to what seemed a dead end, but a little swing of the flashlight showed cracks branching right and left.

"Emma?" he called.

"Here!"

Her voice came from the right, so he moved along that branch. "Emma?"

"Yeah, yeah! What?"

"When I say your name, you're supposed to say 'Here!'"

"I already did that!"

He followed another crack to the left. "Emma?"

There was no answer. Stanley managed a few more feet and then, quite suddenly, the crack widened. He called again. "Emma?"

"Bananas!"

"Keep talking," he shouted. "I need to hear you!"

"Bananas! Here! Blah, blah! Whatever! Hey, I can see your light!"

And there shc was. The crack had widened to become a small cave, at the back of which sat Emma. Her jeans and shirt were smudged with dirt, but it was most surely Emma, squinting against the brightness of his light.

"You!" she exclaimed. "From school! The flattie!"

Don't lose your temper, Stanley told himself. "I was the only one they thought could get in here. How are you doing, Emma?"

Emma rolled her eyes. "Oh, just great! A whole building falls on me, and they send in a flattie! And now I'm starving to death!"

Stanley untaped the slices of bread and cheese, and handed them over.

"Cheese, huh?" Emma put her sandwich together and took a bite. "I hate cheese. Got anything to drink, flattie?"

"Please don't call me flattie. Here." He held out the silver cigarette case.

Emma rolled her eyes again. "I'm not allowed to smoke."

"It's soda."

She opened the cigarette case and sipped. "Blaahh! I hate grape!"

Chief Johnson's voice rose from a hole in the wall behind her. "Stanley? You there yet?"

Emma jerked a thumb at the hole. "It's for you, flattie."

"I'm here, Chief!" Stanley called. "Emma's okay."

He heard cheering, and then the Chief's voice came again. "See a way out, Stan?"

"I haven't had a chance to look around yet. Emma's eating."

"We'll wait. Over and out, Stan!"

"You too!" Stanley called.

He waited until Emma had finished her sandwich. "Emma, how did you get into this mess? What made you come in here?"

"I just came over to look," Emma said. "And they had all these signs! 'Danger! Keep out!' All over the place, even behind in the parking lot.

'Keep out! Danger! Danger!' I really hate that, you know? So there was this door, and it was open, so I went in." She finished the grape soda. "Okay, let's go."

"Not the way I came in," Stanley said. "I could just barely squeeze through. And we have to be careful, because—"

"I know!" Emma interrupted. "Chief whatshisname kept telling me: 'Don't move around! The whole rest of the building might crash down!' So am I supposed to live down here forever?"

"This door you came through," Stanley said. "How far did you come to find this sort of cave we're in?"

"Who said anything about far? I

just got inside, and there were these crashing noises, and the whole building was shaking, and I fell down right here! The crashing went on forever! I thought I was going to die!"

"Calm down." An idea came into Stanley's head. "Just where was this door? Do you remember?"

"Over there somewhere." Emma pointed into the darkness of a corner behind her.

Stanley swung his light, but saw only what seemed to be a solid wall of splintered boards, rock, and brick.

Emma pointed a bit left, then right. "Maybe there . . . I don't know! Was I supposed to take pictures or something?

What difference does it make?"

"We might be just a little bit inside that door," Stanley said. "And what we want is to be just outside of it."

Moving closer to the corner, he saw that a jagged piece of wood protruded at waist level. It came out easily when he tugged, followed by loose dirt.

Emma stood beside him. "Why are you making this mess?"

He poked in the hole with the stick. "Maybe I'll find—"

Dirt cascaded from the wall, covering his shoes. He saw light now, not just the little circle from his flashlight, but daylight! Unmistakably daylight!

"Oooohhhh!" said Emma.

Stanley made the hole still larger, and they saw that a door lay on its side across the bottom of the hole, wreckage limiting the opening on both sides. But it was big enough! They would be able to wiggle through! He ran back to the wall from which Chief Johnson's voice had come.

"We're on our way out!" he shouted. "We'll be in back, in the courtyard!"

"Got it!" came the Chief's voice.

"Great work!"

Stanley turned to Emma. "Let's go!"

"I'll get all dirty, silly," Emma said. "Maybe we could just—"

"Come ON!"

"Don't yell!" Emma said, but she crawled quickly through the hole with Stanley right behind her.

Hero!

There was much rejoicing in the courtyard. Mrs. Lambchop kissed Stanley and Arthur. Mrs. Weeks kissed Emma, and then everyone else, even Flash Tobin, who had arrived to take pictures. Mr. Lambchop shook hands with Mr. Weeks and Chief Johnson, who announced several times that Stanley was a great hero.

Flash Tobin took a group picture of all the Lambchops. "Need one more," he said. "Emma, just you and Stanley. Your hero, right? Saved your life!"

"I could have got out by myself," Emma said. "I just didn't know exactly where the door was." But she went to stand by Stanley.

"Smile!" Flash Tobin took the picture. "Yes, that's good!" He gave Stanley a cheerful slap on the back, just as Emma's elbow jabbed hard into Stanley's ribs.

"Owww!" Stanley yelled.

Emma grinned. "That's for you, Mr. Hero!"

"Are you crazy? What—" Stanley

stopped. Everybody was staring at him. He felt peculiar, as if— Yes! He was getting round again!

"Wow!" Emma said. "How do you do that?"

"Hooray for you, dear!" shouted Mrs. Lambchop, and more cries rose from the others in the courtyard. "Do you see what I see? . . . He's blowing up! . . . Are we crazy or what?"

Flash Tobin aimed his camera again. "Hold it, kid!"

But he was too late. Before him now stood a smiling Stanley Lambchop, shaped like a regular boy!

Mr. Lambchop ran to hug him, and everyone else applauded.

"Been thirty years with the Fire Department, and never saw anything like that!" said Chief Johnson. "Wouldn't have missed it!"

"I'm really glad," Stanley said. "But

what made it happen?"

"What Dr. Dan said!" shouted Arthur. "Remember? The Osteo-posteo-whatever!"

"The OBP! The Osteal Balance Point." Mr. Lambchop smiled. "Yes! The slap on the back from Flash Tobin, and the poke from Emma! That did it!"

A board fell from the tilting roof of the Merker Building, landing in a corner of the courtyard.

"Let's go, folks," said Chief Johnson. "We're not safe here!"

A moment later, back out in the street, there was more hugging and kissing and saying good night. Suddenly, behind them, there were great creaking and grinding sounds. Turning, they watched what was left of the Merker building come crashing down.

Emma spoke first. "Oh, boy," she said softly. "Wow!"

Mrs. Weeks caught her eye, and gave a little nod toward Stanley.

Emma looked puzzled. "Huh? . . . Oh, yeah!" She turned to Stanley. "I guess maybe you, you know, saved my life. Whatever." She kissed his cheek. "Thank you very much, Stanley Lambchop."

"It's okay," Stanley said, quite red in the face. "You're welcome."

Everyone went home.

Fame!

At bedtime the next evening, the Lambchops read again the *Daily Sentinel* they had enjoyed so much at breakfast that morning.

The front page headline read: RUDE GIRL SAVED! FLAT RESCUER REGAINS SHAPE! There were also two Flash Tobin photographs—the Lambchop family picture and the one of Stanley and Emma taken just before she poked him in the ribs. Arthur was particularly pleased with the family picture.

"Finally!" he said. "Not just Stanley! People could have been wondering if he

had a brother, you know? Can I have this one?"

"You may," said Mrs. Lambchop. "I want the one of Stanley with Emma, for my kitchen wall."

"I don't care about pictures," Stanley said. "I just hope I never go back to being flat."

Mrs. Lambchop patted his hand. "I told Dr. Dan of your recovery, dear. He thinks it most unlikely the flatness will occur again."

"Yay!" said Stanley.

Arthur cut the family picture out of the paper, and used a red pencil to draw an arrow, pointing up at him, in the white space at the bottom. Under the arrow, he wrote, *Hero's Brother.* Then he taped the picture to the wall above his bed.

Soon all the Lambchops were asleep.

HERO'S BROTHER

The End

FLAT STANLEY

Stanley in Space

For Sidney Urquhart,
the godmother to whom Flat Stanley owes so much

CONTENTS

"Will you meet with us?
Does anyone hear?"
From the great farness of space,
from farther than any planet or
star that has ever been mentioned
in books, the questions came.
Again and again.
"Will you meet with us?
Does anyone hear?"

The Call

It was Saturday morning, and Mr. and Mrs. Lambchop were putting up wallpaper in the kitchen.

"Isn't this nice, George?" said Mrs. Lambchop, stirring paste. "No excitement. A perfectly *usual* day."

Mr. Lambchop knew just what she meant. Excitement was often troublesome. The flatness of their

1

son Stanley, for example, after his big bulletin board settled on him overnight. Exciting, but worrying too, till Stanley got round again. And that genie visiting, granting wishes. Oh, very exciting! But all the wishes had to be *unwished* before the genie returned to the lamp from which he sprung.

"Yes, dear." Mr. Lambchop smoothed down wallpaper. "Ordinary. The very best sort of day."

In the living room, Stanley Lambchop and his younger brother, Arthur, were watching a Tom Toad cartoon on TV. The sporty Toad was water-skiing and fell off, making a great splash. Arthur

laughed so hard he didn't hear
the telephone, but Stanley
answered it.

"Lambchop residence?"
said the caller. "The
President of the
United States
speaking.
Who's this?"

Stanley smiled. "The
King of France."

"They don't have kings in France.
Not anymore."

"Excuse me, but I'm too busy for
jokes." Stanley kept his eyes on the
TV. "My brother and I are watching

the *Tom Toad Show*."

"Well, you *keep* watching, young fellow!" The caller hung up, just as Mr. and Mrs. Lambchop came in to watch the rest of the show.

"Hey, guess what?" Stanley said.

"Hay is for horses," said Mrs. Lambchop, mindful always of careful speech. "Who called, dear?"

Stanley laughed. "The President of the United States!"

Arthur laughed too. "Stanley

said *he* was the King of France!"

Tom Toad vanished suddenly from the TV screen, and an American flag appeared. "We bring you a special message from the White House in Washington, D.C.," said the deep voice of an announcer. "Ladies and gentlemen, the President of the United States!"

The screen showed the President, looking very serious, behind his desk.

"My fellow Americans," the President said. "I am sorry to interrupt this program, but someone out there doesn't realize that I am a very busy man who can't

waste time joking on the telephone. I hope the particular person I am talking to—and I do *not* mean the King of France!—will remember that. Thank you. Now here's the Toad show again."

Tom Toad, still water-skiing, came back on the TV.

"Stanley!" exclaimed Mrs. Lambchop. "The King of France indeed!"

"Gosh!" Arthur said. "Will Stanley get put in jail?"

"There is no law against being a telephone smarty," Mr. Lambchop said. "Perhaps there should be."

The telephone rang, and he answered it. "George Lambchop here."

"Good!" It was the President. "I've been trying to get hold of you!"

"Oh, my!" Mr. Lambchop said. "Please excuse—"

"Hold on. You're the fellow has the boy was flat once, got his picture in the newspaper?"

"My son Stanley, Mr. President," Mr. Lambchop said, to let the others know who was calling.

"I had to be sure," said the President. "We have to get together, Lambchop! I'll send my private plane right now, fetch you all here to Washington, D.C."

Mr. Lambchop gasped. "Private plane? Washington? *All* of us?"

"The whole family." The President chuckled. "Including the King of France."

Washington

At the White House, in his famous Oval Office, the President shook hands with all the Lambchops.

"Thanks for coming." He chuckled. "Bet you never thought when you woke up this morning that you'd get to meet me."

"Indeed not," Mr. Lambchop said. "This is quite a surprise."

"Well, here's another one," said the President. "The reason I asked you to come."

He sat down behind his desk, serious now. "Tyrra! Never heard of it, right?"

The Lambchops all shook their heads.

"*Nobody* ever heard of it. It's a planet, up there somewhere. They sent a message, the first ever from outer space!"

The Lambchops were greatly interested. "Imagine!" Mrs. Lambchop exclaimed. "What did it say?"

"Very friendly tone," the President said. "Peaceful, just checking around. Asked us to visit. Now, my plan—"

A side door of the Oval Office had opened suddenly to reveal a nicely dressed lady wearing a crown. Mrs. Lambchop recognized her at once as the Queen of England.

"About the banquet, also the—" the Queen began, and saw that the President was busy. "Ooops! We beg your pardon." She closed the door.

"This place is a *madhouse*," the President said. "Visitors, fancy dinners, no end to it. Now, where—? Ah, yes! The *Star Scout*!"

He leaned forward.

"That's our new top-secret spaceship, just ready now! Send somebody up in the *Star Scout*, I thought, to meet with these Tyrrans. But who? Wouldn't look peaceful to send soldiers, or even scientists. Then I thought: What could be more peaceful than just an ordinary American boy?"

The President smiled. "Why not Stanley Lambchop?"

"Stanley?" Mrs. Lambchop gasped. "In a spaceship? To meet with an alien race?"

"Oh, boy!" said Stanley. "I would love to go!"

"Me too," said Arthur. "It's not fair if—"

"Arthur!" Mr. Lambchop drew in a deep breath. "Mr. President, why *Stanley*?"

"It has to be someone who's already had adventure experience," the President said. "Well, my Secret Service showed me a newspaper story about when Stanley was flat and caught two robbers. Robbers! That's adventure!"

"I've had them too!" Arthur said. "A genie taught me to fly, and we had a Liophant, and—"

"A *what*?"

"A Liophant," Arthur said. "Half lion, half elephant. They're nice."

"Is that right? The Secret Service never—"

"Mr. President?" Mrs. Lambchop did not like to interrupt, but her concern was great.

"Mr. President?" she said. "This *mission*: Is it safe?"

"My goodness, of course it's safe!" the President said. "We have taken great care, Mrs. Lambchop. The *Star Scout* has all the latest scientific equipment. And it has been very carefully tested. First, we tried it on automatic pilot, with no passengers. It worked perfectly! Even then, ma'am, we were not satisfied. We sent the *Star Scout* up again, this time with our cleverest trained bird aboard. But hear for yourself." The President spoke into a little box on his desk. "Send in Dr. Schwartz, please."

A bearded man entered, wearing a white coat and carrying a birdcage with a cloth over it. Bowing, he removed the cloth to reveal a large, brightly colored parrot.

"Thank you, Herman," the President said. "Dr. Schwartz is our top space scientist," he told the Lambchops, "and this is Polly, the bird I spoke of. Polly, tell the folks here about your adventure into space."

"Piece of cake," said the parrot. "Terrific! Loved every minute of it!"

"Thank you, Herman," the President said, and Dr. Schwartz carried Polly away.

"That was very reassuring, but it is out of the question for Stanley to go alone," Mrs. Lambchop said. "However,

we were planning a family vacation. Would it be possible, Mr. President, for us all to go?"

"Well, if you didn't mind the crowding," the President said. "And skimping on baggage."

"Actually, we had in mind the seaside," Mr. Lambchop said. "Or a tennis camp. But—"

The Queen of England looked in again. "May we ask if—"

"Just a *minute*, for heaven's sake!" said the President.

"We shall return anon." Looking peeved, the Queen went away.

Mr. Lambchop had decided. "Mr. President, the seaside will keep. We will go to Tyrra, sir."

"Wonderful!" The President jumped up. "To the stars, Lambchops! Some training at the Space Center, and you're on your way!"

Taking Off

"Ten!" said the voice of Mission Control.

The countdown had begun. When it reached "zero," Chief Pilot Stanley Lambchop would press the "Start" button, and the *Star Scout* would blast off for Tyrra.

"Nine!"

Strapped into their seats, the

Lambchops held their breaths, each thinking very different thoughts.

Stanley was wondering if the Tyrrans would mind that Earth had sent just an ordinary family. Suppose they were big stuck-ups and expected a general or a TV star, or even the President? Suppose—

"Eight!" said Control, and Stanley fixed his eyes on the panel before him.

Mr. Lambchop was thinking that serving one's country was noble, but this was a bit much. How did these things happen? Off to an unknown planet, the entire family! Other families didn't have a son become flat. Other families didn't find genies in the house. Other— Oh, well! Mr. Lambchop sighed.

"Seven!" said Control.

Mrs. Lambchop thought that Mr. Lambchop seemed fretful. But why, now that the *Star Scout* looked so *nice*? Thanks to her, in fact. "They may call it a spaceship," she had said when she first saw it, "but where's the *space*? Just one room! And all gray . . . ? Drab, I say!" Much of the training at the Space Center, however, was physical, and Mrs. Lambchop, who jogged and exercised regularly, quickly passed the tests required. In the days that followed, while the others were being made fit, she used her free time to make the *Star Scout* more like home. Only so much weight was permitted, but she managed a bathroom scale for the shower alcove and a plastic curtain, pretty shades for the portholes, a venetian blind for the Magnifying Exploration Window, and posters of Mexico and France.

"Six! . . . Five! . . . Four! . . . Three! . . ."

Mrs. Lambchop made sure her purse was snug beneath her seat.

Arthur, by nature lazy, was thinking that he was glad to be done with all the jogging, jumping, climbing ladders, and scaling walls. When he was super-strong, thanks to the genie, it would have been easy. But for just plain Arthur Lambchop, he thought, it was tiring.

"Two!" said Control. "Good luck, everybody! One!"

"Pay attention, dear," Mrs. Lambchop told Stanley.

"Zero!" said Control, and Stanley pressed the "Start" button.

Whrooom! Rockets roaring, the *Star Scout* rose from its launching pad.

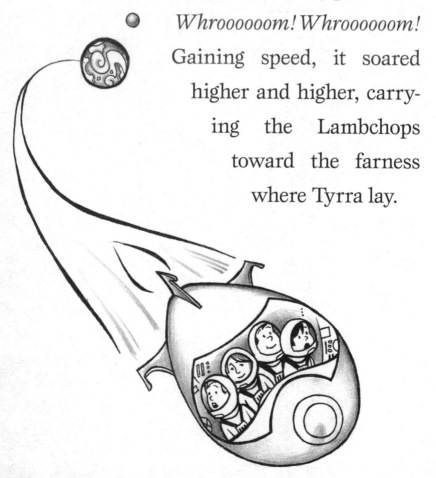

Whroooooom! Whroooooom! Gaining speed, it soared higher and higher, carrying the Lambchops toward the farness where Tyrra lay.

In Space

"I'll just flip this omelette," said Mrs. Lambchop, making breakfast in the *Star Scout*, "and then— Oh, dear!" The omelette hovered like a Frisbee in the air above her.

Mostly, however, after weeks in space, the Lambchops remembered that gravity, the force that held things down, did not exist beyond Earth's

atmosphere. Mr. Lambchop often read now with his hands clasped behind his head, allowing his book to float before him, and Stanley and Arthur greatly enjoyed pushing from their chairs to drift like feathers across the room.

Raising her pan, Mrs. Lambchop brought down the omelette. "After breakfast, what?" she said. "A game of Monopoly?"

"Please, not again." Arthur sighed. "If I'd known this adventure would be so boring, I'd never have come."

"The worst part," Stanley said, "is not knowing how long it will last."

"The beginning wasn't boring," Arthur said as they began their breakfast. "The beginning was fun."

The first days had in fact been tremendously exciting. They had spent many hours at the *Star Scout*'s Magnifying Window, watching the bright globe of Earth grow steadily smaller, until it seemed at last only a pale marble in the black of space. And there had been many special sights to see: the starry beauty of the Milky Way, the planets—red Mars, giant Jupiter, cloudy Venus, Saturn with its shining rings.

The third evening they appeared on TV news broadcasts on Earth. Word of their voyage had been released to the press, and all over the world people were eager to learn how this extraordinary adventure was proceeding. Standing before the spaceship's camera, the Lambchops said they felt fine, looked forward to meeting the Tyrrans, and would report nightly while they remained in TV range.

The fourth evening they floated before the camera, demonstrating weightlessness. This was greatly appreciated on Earth, and they floated again the following day.

By the sixth evening, however, they were hard-pressed to liven their appearances. Mr. Lambchop recited a baseball poem, "Casey at the Bat."

Stanley juggled tennis balls, but the Earth audience, knowing now about weightlessness, saw the balls float when he tossed them up. Arthur did imitations

of a rooster, a dog, and a man stuck in a phone booth. After this, while Mrs. Lambchop was singing her college song, he went behind the plastic curtain to undress for a shower and accidentally pulled the curtain down. He was mortified, and she tried later to comfort him.

"We will be remembered, Arthur, for our time in space," she said. "Nobody will care about a curtain."

"I will be remembered *forever*," Arthur said. "A hundred million people saw me in my underwear."

The next day was Stanley's birthday, and just after dinner the screen lit up. There was the President in his shirtsleeves, behind his desk in Washington, D.C.

"Well, here I am working late again," the President said. "It's a tough job, believe me. Happy birthday, Stanley Lambchop! I've arranged a surprise. First, your friends from school."

There was silence for a moment, broken only by the clearing of throats, and then, from all the millions of miles away, came the voices of Stanley's classmates singing, "Happy Birthday, dear Stanley! Happy Birthday to you!"

Stanley was tremendously pleased. "Thanks, everybody!" he said. "You too, Mr. President."

"That was just the U.S.A. part," said

the President. "Ready over there in London, Queen?"

"We are indeed," the Queen's voice said cheerfully. "And now, Master Lambchop, our famous Westminster Boys' Choir!"

From England, the beautiful voices of the famous choir sang "Happy Birthday, Stanley!" all over again, and then other children sang it from Germany, Spain, and France.

All this attention to Stanley made Arthur jealous, and when the President said, "By the way, Arthur, you entertained us wonderfully the other night," he was sure this was a tease about his appearance in underwear.

But he was wrong.

"Those imitations!" the President said. "Especially the fellow in the phone booth. Darn good!"

"Indeed!" the Queen added from England. "We were greatly amused."

"Oh, thank you!" said Arthur, cheered. "I—"

The screen had gone blank.

They had traveled too far. There would be no more voices from Earth, no voices but their own until they heard what the Tyrrans had to say.

"Suppose the Tyrrans have forgotten we're coming?" Stanley said. "We might just sail around in space *forever*."

They had finished the breakfast omelette, and were now setting out the Monopoly board because there was nothing more interesting to do.

"They don't even know our names," Arthur said. "What will they call us?"

"Earth people!" said a deep voice.

"Very probably," said Mr. Lambchop. "'Earth people' seems— Who said that?"

"Not me," said both Stanley and Arthur.

"Not *I*," said Mrs. Lambchop, correcting. "But who—"

"Earth people!" The voice, louder now, came from the *Star Scout*'s radio. "Greetings from the great planet Tyrra and its mighty people! Do you hear?"

"Oh, my!" Mr. Lambchop turned up the volume. "It's them!"

"They," said Mrs. Lambchop.

"For heaven's sake, Harriet!" Mr. Lambchop said, and spoke loudly into the microphone. "Hello, Tyrra. Earth people here. Party of four. Peace-loving family."

"Peace-loving?" said the voice. "Good! So is mighty Tyrra! Where are you, Earth people?"

Stanley checked his star maps. "We're just where the tail of Ralph's Comet meets star number three million and forty-seven. Now what?"

"Right," said the Tyrran voice. "Keep

going till you pass a star formation that looks like a foot. You can't miss it. Then, just past a lopsided little white moon, start down. You'll see a pointy mountain, then a big field. Land there. See you soon, Earth people!"

"You bet!" Mr. Lambchop said, and turned to his family. "The first contact with another planet! We are making history!"

They passed the foot-shaped star formation, then the lopsided moon, and Stanley piloted the *Star Scout* down. The darkness of space vanished as it descended, and at last the Lambchops saw clearly the planet it had taken so long to reach.

Tyrra was smallish as planets go, but nicely round and quite pretty, all in shades of brown with markings not unlike the oceans and continents of Earth. A pointy mountain came into sight, and beyond it a big field.

"There!" Stanley pressed the "Landing" button.

Whrooom! went the *Star Scout*'s rockets. The spaceship hovered, then touched down.

Peering out, the Lambchops saw only a brown field, with tan trees at the far side and brownish hills beyond.

"Curious," said Mr. Lambchop. "Where are—"

Suddenly a message came, but not the sort they expected.

"Surrender, Earth people!" said the radio. "Your spaceship is trapped by our unbreakable trapping cable! You are prisoners of Tyrra! Surrender!"

The Tyrrans

Unbreakable trapping cable? Prisoners? Surrender? The Lambchops could scarcely believe their ears.

"I don't call *that* peaceful," said Mrs. Lambchop. "Our President has been misled."

"I wish we had gone to the seaside." Mr. Lambchop shook his head. "But *how* are we trapped? I don't—" He pointed to the Magnifying Window. "What's that?"

A thin blue line, like a thread, had been passed over the *Star Scout*. Stanley switched on the wiper above the big window and the first flick of its blade parted the blue line.

"Drat!" said the radio.

Other voices rose, startled, and then the deep voice spoke again. "Earth people! We're sending a messenger! A regular, ordinary Tyrran, just to show what we're like."

For long moments, the Lambchops kept their eyes on the tan trees across the field.

"There!" Arthur said suddenly.

"Coming toward— Oh! Oh, my . . ." His voice trailed away.

The Tyrran messenger came slowly forward to stand before the big window, a muscular, scowling young man with a curling mustache, wearing shorts and carrying a club.

The mustache was very large. The messenger was not.

"That man," Mrs. Lambchop said slowly, "is only three inches tall."

"At most," Mr. Lambchop said. "It is a magnifying window."

The Tyrran seemed to be calling something. Arthur opened the door a crack, and the words came clearly now. ". . . afraid to let us see you, Earth

people? Because I'm so enormous? Hah! *All* Tyrrans are this big!"

Flinging the door wide, Arthur showed himself. "Well, I'm a *small* Earth person!" he shouted. "The rest are even bigger than me!"

"*I*, not me," Mrs. Lambchop said. "And don't tease, Arth— Oh! He's fainted!"

Wetting her handkerchief with cold water, she jumped down from the *Star Scout* and ran to dab the Tyrran's tiny brow.

Cries rose again from the spaceship's radio. "A giant killed Ik! . . . There's another, even bigger! . . . Oh, gross! . . . Look! Ik's all right!"

The Tyrran, by grasping Mrs. Lambchop's handkerchief, had indeed pulled himself up. Furious, he swung his club, but managed only to tap the top of her shoe. "Ouch! Scat!" she said, and he darted back across the field.

"Oh, my!" said the radio. "Never mind about surrendering, Earth people! A truce committee is on the way!"

At first they saw only a tiny flag, fluttering like a white butterfly far across the brown field, but at last the Tyrran committee drew close, and the Lambchops, waiting now outside the *Star Scout*, could make each little person out.

The flag was carried by the scowling

young man with the mustache and the club. The other members of the committee, a bit smaller even than he, were a red-faced man wearing a uniform with medals across the chest, a stout lady in a yellow dress and a hat with flowers on it, and two older men

in blue suits, one with wavy white hair, the other thin and bald.

The committee halted, staring bravely up.

"I am General Ap!" shouted the uniformed man. "Commander of all Tyrran forces!"

Stanley stepped forward. "Chief Pilot Stanley Lambchop," he said. "From Earth. These are my parents, Mr. and Mrs. George Lambchop. And my brother, Arthur."

"President Ot of Tyrra, and Mrs. Ot," said General Ap, indicating the wavy-haired man and the lady. "The bald chap is Dr. Ep, our Chief Scientist. The grouchy one with the flag is my aide, Captain Ik."

No one seemed sure what to say next. A few polite remarks were exchanged—"Nice meeting you, Earth people!" . . . "Such a pretty planet, Tyrra!" . . . "Thank you. Were you very long in space?"—and Mr. Lambchop realized suddenly that the Tyrrans were uncomfortable talking almost straight up. He got down on his knees, the other Lambchops following his example, and the Tyrrans at once lowered their heads in relief.

"Right!" said General Ap. "All reasonable people here! A truce, eh?"

"I'm for war, frankly," growled

Captain Ik, but Stanley pretended not to hear. "A truce? Good idea," he said. "We come in peace."

Mrs. Ot sniffed. "Not very peaceful, frightening poor Captain Ik." She pointed at Arthur. "That giant shouted at him!"

"My son is not a giant," Mrs. Lambchop said. "It's just that you Tyrrans are—how to put it?—unusually *petite.*"

"Ik's the biggest we've got, actually," said General Ap. "We hoped he'd scare you."

President Ot raised his hand. "No harm done! Come! TyrraVille, our capital, is but a stroll away."

The Lambchops, equipped now with handy magnifying lenses from the *Star Scout*'s science kit, followed the committee.

TyrraVille lay just across the brown field, behind the tan trees, no larger than an Earth-size tennis court.

TyrraVille

"Gosh!" Stanley said. "It makes me homesick, in a way."

Except for its size, and the lack of greenness, the Tyrran capital was indeed much like a small village on Earth. A Main Street bustled with Tyrrans shopping and running errands; there were handsome school and public buildings, two churches with spires as high as Mr. Lambchop's waist, and side streets of pretty houses with lawns like neat brown postage stamps.

Captain Ik, still angry, marched on ahead, but the rest of the committee halted at the head of Main Street.

"We'll just show you *around*, eh?" said President Ot. "Safer, I think."

The Lambchops saw at once the risk of walking streets scarcely wider than their feet. Escorted by the committee, they circled the little capital, bending often to make use of their magnifying lenses. Mrs. Ot took care to indicate points of particular interest, among them Ux Field, a sports center, Admiral Ux Square, Ux Park, and the Ux

Science Center Building. ("Mrs. Ot's grandfather," whispered General Ap. "Very rich!")

The tour caused a great stir. Everywhere the tiny citizens of TyrraVille waved from windows and rooftops. At the Science Center, the last stop, journalists took photographs, and the Lambchops were treated to Grape Fizzola, the Tyrran national drink, hundreds of bottles of which were emptied into four tubs to make Earth-size portions.

Refreshed by his Fizzola, Arthur took a little run and hurdled a large part of TyrraVille, landing in Ux Square. "Arthur!" Mrs. Lambchop scolded, and he hurdled back.

"Aren't kids the dickens?" said a Tyrran mother, looking on. "Mine— Stop *tugging*, Herbert!" These last words seemed addressed to the ground beside her. "My youngest," she explained.

Stanley squinted. "I can hardly— He's just a *dot*."

"Dot yourself!" said an angry voice. "Big-a-rooney! *You're* the funny-looking one!"

"Herbert!" his mother said. "It is

57

rude to make fun of people for their shape or size!"

"As I said myself, often, when Stanley was flat!" Mrs. Lambchop exclaimed. "If only—"

"Surrender, Earth people!"

The cry had come from Captain Ik, who appeared now from behind the Science Center, staggering beneath the weight of a boxlike machine almost as big as he was, with a tube sticking out of it.

"Surrender!" he shouted. "You cannot resist our Magno-Titanic Paralyzer Ray! Tyrra will yet be saved!"

"There's a truce, Ik!" barked General Ap. "You can't—"

"Yes, I can! First— Ooops!" Captain Ik's knees had buckled, but he recovered himself. "First I'll paralyze the one who scared me back there in the field!"

Yellow light flickered up at Arthur from the Magno-Titanic Paralyzer.

"Yikes!" said Arthur, as shrieks rose from the crowd.

But it was not on Arthur that the Magno-Titanic beam landed. Stanley had sprung forward to protect his brother, and the light shone now on his chest and shoulders. Mrs. Lambchop almost fainted.

Suddenly her fright was gone.

Stanley was smiling. The yellow rays still flickering upon him, he rolled his head and wiggled his hands to show that he was fine. "It's nice, actually," he said. "Like a massage."

The crowd hooted. "It only works on people Tyrran-size!" someone called. "You're a ninny, Ik!" Then Captain Ik was marched off by a Tyrran policeman, and the crowd, still laughing, drifted away.

Mrs. Lambchop spoke sternly to the committee. "'Tyrra will yet be saved'? What did Captain Ik mean? And why, pray tell, did he attempt to paralyze my son?"

The Ots and General Ap exchanged glances. Dr. Ep stared at the ground.

"Ah!" said President Ot. "Well . . .

The fact is, we're having a . . . A crisis, actually. Yes. And Ik, well, he, ah—"

"Oh, tell them!" Mrs. Ot burst suddenly into tears. "About the Super-Gro! Tell, for heaven's sake!"

Puzzled, the Lambchops stared at her. The sky had darkened, and now a light rain began to fall.

"Wettish, eh?" said General Ap. "Can't offer shelter, I'm afraid. No place large enough."

"The *Star Scout* will do nicely," said Mrs. Lambchop. "Let us return to it for tea."

President Ot's Story

"Tea *does* help. I am quite myself again."
Mrs. Ot nodded to her husband. "Go
on, dear. Tell."

Rain drummed faintly on the *Star
Scout*, making even cozier the scene
within. Around the dining table,
the Lambchops occupied their usual
places. The Tyrrans sat atop the table
on thumbtacks pushed down to serve

as stools, sipping from tiny cups Mrs. Lambchop had fashioned from aluminum foil, and nibbling crumbs of her homemade ginger snaps.

Now, sighing, President Ot set down his cup.

"You will have observed, Lamb-chops," he said, "how greatly we have enjoyed these tasty refreshments. The fact is, Tyrra has for some time been totally without fresh food or water fit to drink. We live now only by what tins and bottles we had in store."

Mrs. Ot made a face. "Pink meat spreads, and spinach. And that *dreadful* Fizzola."

"A bit sweet, yes," said General Ap.

"Gives one gas, too. But—"

"Never mind!" cried Mrs. Ot.

President Ot continued. "The cause of our tragedy, Lambchops, was Super-Gro. An invention of Dr. Ep's. Super-Gro, Ep promised, would double our crops, make them double size, double delicious as well. A great concept, he said."

"We scientists," said Dr. Ep, "dream larger than other men."

"For three days, at the Science Center," President Ot went on, "Ep brewed his Super-Gro. Great smelly vats of it, enough for the whole planet. But then . . . Oh, no Tyrran will ever forget that fourth day! I myself was strolling through Ux Park. How beautiful it was! The trees and grass so green, the sky—"

"Green?" said Arthur. "But everything's *brown* here, not green!"

"A mishap," murmured Dr. Ep. "With the Super-Gro."

"Mishap?" barked General Ap. "The stuff *exploded*, Ep! All over the place!"

"Well, nobody's perfect." Dr. Ep hung his head.

"All those huge vats, Lambchops!" President Ot continued. "Boom! One after another! Shattered windows, blew the roof off the Science Center! No one hurt, thank goodness, but great clouds of smoke, darkening the sky! And then—such dreadful luck!—it began to rain. A *tremendous* rain, mixing with the smoke, falling all over Tyrra, into the rivers, on to every field and garden, every bit of greenery."

Rising from his thumbtack, he paced back and forth across the table.

"When the rain stopped, there was no green. None. Just brown. Worse, Ep's tests proved that our water was undrinkable, and that nowhere on Tyrra would anything grow. I broadcast at once to the nation. 'Do not despair,' I said, 'Tyrra will soon recover.'"

"Oh, good!" Mr. Lambchop said.

President Ot shook his head. "I lied. I couldn't tell the truth, for fear of causing panic, you see. The tests showed that it would be a year at least before Tyrra was green again. And long before that we will have emptied our last tin, our last bottle of Fizzola."

He sat down again, covering his face with his hands.

"So then we . . . We sent a message, into space. Lure some other planet's spaceship, we thought. Hold it for ransom, you see, make them send food and water. Oh, shameful! Underhanded. You will never forgive us, I know . . ."

His voice trailed away, and there was only the patter of the rain.

Close to tears, the Lambchops looked at each other, then at the little people on the tabletop. The Tyrrans seemed particularly tiny now, and brave, and nice.

"You poor dears!" Mrs. Lambchop said. "There was no need to *conquer* us. We would help you willingly, if we could."

The Tyrrans seemed at first unable to believe their ears. Then, suddenly, their faces shone with joy.

"Bless you!" cried General Ap.

"Saved!" Mrs. Ot clapped her hands. "We are saved!"

"Saved . . . ?" said Mrs. Lambchop.

"Of course!" said President Ot. "Don't you see? Earth's spaceships can bring food and water till— Oh! What's wrong?"

It was Arthur who explained.

"I'm very sorry," he said. "But there's just the *Star Scout*. Earth hasn't got any other spaceships. And it would take years to build them."

The Tyrrans gasped. "Years . . . ?" said Dr. Ep.

Stanley felt so sad he could hardly speak. "And it's no use going for food in the *Star Scout*," he said. "By the time we returned from Earth, you'd all be— Well, you know."

"Dead," said Mrs. Ot.

In the *Star Scout*, a terrible silence fell. The facts were clear. The cupboards of Tyrra would soon be empty. And then all its tiny people would starve to death.

Stanley's Good Idea

The teapot was cold now, and a last cookie crumb lay unwanted on a plate. Gloom hung like a dark cloud within the *Star Scout*.

"It's not fair," Arthur said for the third time. "It's just not."

"Stop saying that," Stanley told him. "That's four times now."

"Five," said Dr. Ep.

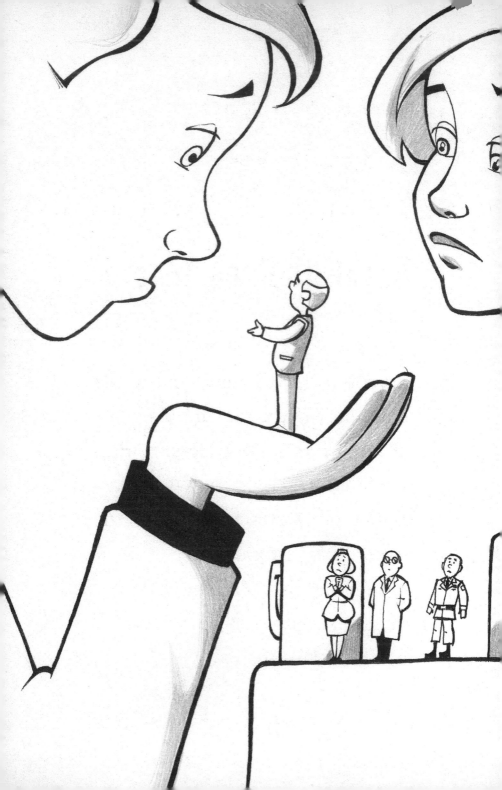

General Ap tried to be cheerful. "Ah, well . . . Still some tinned meat, eh? And plenty of Grape Fizzola. Much to be thankful for."

"I will *never* be thankful for Grape Fizzola," said Mrs. Ot.

"It's just that . . ." Arthur sighed. "I mean, Earth has so *much* food. Millions of people, and there's mostly still enough."

The Tyrrans seemed amazed. "Millions? You're joking?" said President Ot.

"Hah!" said General Ap. "Dreadful crush, I should think. Millions?"

Mrs. Lambchop smiled. "With all our great nations, many millions. And still the numbers grow."

"Well, here too." President Ot shook his head. "Youthful marriages, babies one after another. But *millions*? Our population—there's just TyrraVille, of course—is six hundred and eighty-three."

"Eighty-four," said Mrs. Ot. "Mrs. Ix had a baby last night."

Now it was the Lambchops who were amazed.

"Just TyrraVille?" Arthur cried. "But TyrraVille's your *capital*, you said!"

"Well, it would have to be, wouldn't it, dear?" said Mrs. Ot.

Stanley shook his head. "On the whole planet, only six hundred and

eighty-four Tyrrans! Gosh, I'll bet—
Wait!"

An idea had come to him. Stanley
had had exciting ideas before, but none
that excited him as this one did.

"Mrs. Ot!" he shouted. "How much
do you weigh?"

"Stanley!" said Mrs. Lambchop.

Mrs. Ot was not offended. "Actually, I've slimmed a bit. Though not, sadly, in the hips. I'm six ounces, young man. Why do you ask?"

The words rushed out of Stanley. "Because if you're average, only children would be even lighter, then all the Tyrrans put together would weigh— Let me figure this out!"

"Less than three hundred pounds," said Mr. Lambchop, who was good at math. "Though I don't see—" Then he did see. "Oh! Good for you, Stanley!"

"The lad's bright, we know," said General Ap. "But what—"

"General!" said Mr. Lambchop.

"Summon all Tyrrans here to the *Star Scout*! Fetch what remains of your tinned food and Grape Fizzola! Perhaps Earth can be your home till Tyrra is green again!"

The Weighing

From each little house on each little street, the Tyrrans came, every man, woman, and child, even Captain Ik with a guard from the jail. The rain had stopped, and the evening light shone gold on the brown field in which the tiny people stood assembled.

President Ot addressed them. "Fellow Tyrrans! I must confess that your government has deceived you! The truth is: It will be at least a year before our fields and streams are fit again."

Cries rose from the crowd. "We were lied to!" . . . "Lordy, talk about bad news!" . . . "We'll starve!" . . . "Shoot the scientists!"

"Wait!" shouted President Ot. "We are offered refuge on Earth, if the voyage is possible! Pay attention, please!"

Stepping forward, Mr. Lambchop read aloud from the booklet that had come with the *Star Scout*.

"'Your spacecraft has been designed for safety as well as comfort. Use only as directed.'" He raised his voice. "'Do not add weight by bringing souvenirs aboard *or by inviting friends to ride with you.*'"

Cries rose again. "That did it!" . . . "We're not *souvenirs*!" . . . "He said no friends either, stupid!" . . . "We've had it, looks like!"

Mr. Lambchop raised his hand. "There is still hope! But you must all be weighed! Also the supplies you would require for the trip!"

The *Star Scout*'s bathroom scale, set down in the field, proved too high for the Tyrrans, and the weighing was briefly delayed until Arthur, using the Monopoly board, made a ramp by which they could easily mount.

General Ap barked orders. "Right,

then! Groups of twenty to twenty-five, families together! And don't jiggle!"

The Ots and six other families marched up onto the scale, beside which Mrs. Lambchop stood with pad and pencil. "Seven and one-quarter pounds!" she said, writing it down.

"Next!" shouted General Ap, but the Ot group was already starting down, and another marching up.

Group after group mounted the scale. There *was* jiggling, due to excited children, but Mrs. Lambchop took care to wait until the needle was still. Within an hour the entire population of Tyrra had been weighed, along with its supplies of tinned food and Fizzola, and she added up.

"Tyrrans, two hundred and thirty-nine," she announced. "Food and Fizzola, one hundred and forty. Total: Three hundred and seventy-nine pounds!"

"Are we saved? Or are we too fat?" came a cry.

"Too soon to tell!" Mr. Lambchop called back. "We must see how we can lighten our ship!"

A good start was made by discarding the *Star Scout*'s dining table and one steel bunk, since Stanley and Arthur could easily share. Then out went Stanley's tennis balls, extra sweater, and his Chief Pilot zip jacket with the American flag; out went Arthur's knee socks, raincoat, and a plastic gorilla he had smuggled aboard. Mr. and Mrs. Lambchop added their extra clothing, lamps, kitchenware, the Monopoly game, and at last, the posters of Mexico and France.

The crowd stood hushed as the pile was weighed. Somewhere a baby cried, and its parents scolded it.

"Three hundred and seventy-seven pounds!" Mrs. Lambchop announced. "Oh, dear!" she whispered to President Ot. "Two less than we need."

"I see." President Ot, after a moment's thought, climbed up onto the scale. "Good news, Tyrrans!" he called. "Almost all of us are saved!"

Cheers went up, and then someone shouted, "What do you mean, *almost* all?"

"We weigh, as a nation, a bit too much," President Ot explained. "But only four, if largish, need stay behind. I shall be one. Will three more volunteer?"

Murmurs rose from the crowd. "That's *my* kind of President!" . . . "Leave Ik behind!" . . . "How about you, Ralph?" . . . "Ask somebody else, darn you!"

The matter was quickly resolved. "I won't go without you, dear," Mrs. Ot told her husband, and Captain Ik, hoping to regain popularity, announced that he too would remain.

General Ap was the fourth volunteer. "Just an old soldier, ma'am," he told Mrs. Lambchop. "Lived a full life, time now to just fade away, to—"

"Hey! Wait!"

Arthur was pointing to the scale.

"We forgot *that*," he said. "We can leave the scale behind. Now nobody has to stay!"

Heading Home

"Mr. and Mrs. Ix, and the new baby?" said President Ot, beside his wife on a ledge above the Magnifying Window. "Ah, yes, on the fridge!"

The people of Tyrra were being made as comfortable as possible in the various nooks and crannies of the *Star Scout*. Stanley and Arthur had cleared

a cupboard where Tyrra High School students could study during the trip, and Mrs. Lambchop had cut up sheets to make hundreds of little blankets, and put out bits of cotton for pillows. "Makeshift, Mrs. Ix," she said now, settling the Ixes on the fridge. "But *such* short notice. Back a bit from the edge, yes?"

"Short notice indeed," said Mrs. Ix. "So many—"

"Not to worry." Mrs. Lambchop smiled proudly. "My son, the Chief Pilot, will call ahead."

From a nearby shelf, Captain Ik whispered an apology for attempting to paralyze Arthur. "Between you and I, I didn't really think it would work," he said.

"Between you and *me*," said Mrs. Lambchop. "But thank you, Captain Ik." She turned to Stanley. "We're all ready, dear!"

Stanley checked his controls. "Let's go!"

"Tyrrans!" President Ot called for attention. "Our national anthem!"

Everywhere in the *Star Scout*, Tyrrans rose, their right hands over their hearts. *"Hmmmm . . ."* hummed Mrs. Ot, setting a key, and they began to sing.

"Tyrra, the lovely! Tyrra, the free!
Hear, dear planet, our promise to
thee!
Where e'er we may go, where e'er we
may roam,
We'll come back to Tyrra, Tyrra
our home!"

The words echoed in the softly lit cabin. Many Tyrrans were weeping, and the eyes of the Lambchops, as they took their seats, glistened too.

"Be it ever so humble, there's no
planet so dear,

*We'll always love Tyrra, from far or
from—"*

Stanley pressed the "Start" button,
and—*Whroooom!*—the *Star Scout*'s
rockets roared to life.

The singing stopped suddenly, and
Mrs. Ix cried out from the fridge. "Oh,
my! Is this thing safe?"

"Yes indeed," Mrs. Lambchop called
back.

"Perhaps," said Mrs. Ix. "But it is my
belief that if Tyrrans were meant to fly,
we'd have wings."

Whroooom! Whroooom!

The *Star Scout* lifted now, gaining

speed as it rose. Its mission was done. The strangers who had called from a distant planet were no longer strangers, but friends.

It was all very satisfactory, Stanley thought. The other Lambchops thought so too.

Earth Again

". . . real pleasure to welcome you, Tyrrans," said the President, almost done with his speech. "I wish you a fine year on Earth!"

Before him on the White House lawn, with newspaper and TV reporters all about, sat the Lambchops and, in a tiny grandstand built especially for the

SEAL OF THE PRESIDENT OF THE UNITED STATES

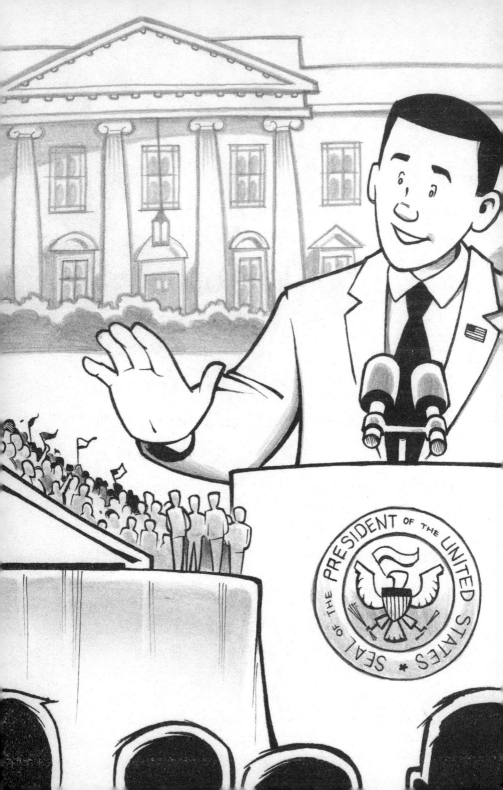

occasion, the people of Tyrra.

The Tyrrans were now applauding politely, but they looked nervous, and Mrs. Lambchop guessed why. That crowd at the Space Center for the *Star Scout*'s landing, that drive through crowded streets into Washington, D.C.! Poor Tyrrans! Everywhere they looked, giant buildings, giant people. How could they feel comfortable here?

But a surprise was in store. Across the lawn, a great white sheet had been spread. Now, at the President's signal, workmen pulled the sheet away.

"Welcome," said the President, "to TyrraVille Two!"

Gasps rose from the Tyrrans, then shouts of joy.

Before them, on what had been the White House tennis court, lay an entire village of tiny houses, one for each Tyrran family, with shops and schools and churches, and a miniature railway serving all principal streets. Begun when Stanley called ahead from space, TyrraVille Two had been completed well before the *Star Scout*'s arrival, thanks to rush deliveries from leading toy stores in Washington and New York.

The excited Tyrrans ran from the grandstand to explore their new homes, and soon happy voices rose from every window and doorway of TyrraVille Two. "Nice furniture!" . . . "Hooray! Fresh lemonade! No more Fizzola!" . . . "In the cupboards, see? Shirts, dresses, suits, shoes!" . . . "Underwear, even!"

The Ots, General Ap, Dr. Ep, and Captain Ik came back to say good-bye, and the Lambchops knelt to touch fingertips in farewell. The TV men filmed this, and Arthur made everyone laugh, pretending to be paralyzed by the touch of Captain Ik. Then the newsmen left, the Tyrrans returned to TyrraVille Two, and only the President remained with the Lambchops on the White House lawn.

"Well, back to work." The President

sighed. "Good-bye, Lambchops. You're all heroes, you know. Saved the nation."

"Not really," Stanley said. "They couldn't have conquered us."

"Well, you know what I mean," the President said. "You folks care to stay for supper?"

"Thank you, no," Mrs. Lambchop said. "It is quite late, and this has been an exciting but very tiring day."

It was bedtime when they got home. Stanley and Arthur had a light supper, with hot chocolate to help them sleep, after which Mr. and Mrs. Lambchop tucked them in and said good night.

The brothers lay quietly in the

darkness for a moment. Then Arthur chuckled.

"The Magno-Titanic Paralyzer *was* sort of scary," he said. "You were brave, Stanley, protecting me."

"That's okay," Stanley said. "You're my brother, right?"

"I know . . ." Arthur was sleepy now. "Stanley? When the Tyrrans go back, will their land and water be okay? Will they let us know?"

"I guess so." Stanley was drowsy too. "Good night, Arthur."

"Good night," said Arthur, and soon they were both asleep.

And in time, from the great
farness of space, but a farness no
longer strange or unknown,
another message came.

"We are home. All is well."
And again.
*"We are home! Thank you, Earth!
All is well!"*

The End

FLAT STANLEY

Stanley and the
Magic Lamp

For Elizabeth Tobin
—J.B.

CONTENTS

Prologue

Once upon a very long time ago, way before the beginning of today's sort of people, there was a magical kingdom in which everyone lived forever, and anyone of importance was a genie, mostly the friendly kind. The few wicked genies kept out of sight in caves or at the bottoms of rivers. They had no wish to provoke the great Genie King, who ruled from a palace with many towers and courtyards and gardens with reflecting pools.

The Genie King was noted for his patience with the high-spirited genie princes of the kingdom, but the Genie Queen thought he was much *too* patient with them. She said so one morning in the throne room, where the King was studying reports and proposals for new magic spells.

"Discipline, that's what they need!" She adjusted the Magic Mirror on the throne room wall. "Florts and collibots! Granting wishes, which they'll be doing one day, is serious work."

"Florts yourself! You're too hard on the lads," said the King, and then he frowned. "However, this report here says that one of them has been behaving very badly indeed."

"Haraz, right?" said the Queen. "He's a *real* smarty!"

The Genie King sent a thought to summon Prince Haraz, which is all such a ruler has to do when he wants somebody, and a moment later the young genie flew into the throne room, did a triple flip, and hovered in

the air before
the throne.

"What's
up?" he asked,
grinning.

"You are!"
said the Queen. "Come down here!"

"No problem," said Haraz,
landing.

"It seems you have been playing
a great many magical jokes," said
the King, tapping the reports before
him. "Very *annoying* jokes, such as
causing the army's carpets to fly only
in circles, which made all my soldiers
dizzy."

"That was a good one!" laughed Haraz.

"And turning the Chief Wizard's wand into a sausage, while he was casting a major spell? You did that?"

"Ha, ha! You should have seen his face!"

"Stop laughing!" cried the Queen. "This is shameful! You should be severely punished!"

"He's just a boy, dear, only two hundred years old," said the King. "But I'll—"

"Who knows what more he's done?" The Queen turned to the Magic Mirror. "Mirror, what other

dumb jokes has Haraz played?"

The Magic Mirror squirted apple juice all over her face and the front of her dress.

"Ooooohh!" The Queen whirled around. "Florts and collibots! I know who's responsible for that!"

Prince Haraz tried to look sorry, but

it was too late.

"That does it!" said the Genie King. "Lamp duty for you, you rascal! One thousand years of service to a lamp." He turned to the Queen. "How's that, my dear?"

"Make it two thousand," said the Queen, drying her face.

Prince Haraz

Almost a year had passed since Stanley Lambchop had gotten over being flat, which he had become when his big bulletin board had settled on him during the night. It had been a pleasant, restful time for all the Lambchops, as this particular evening was.

Dinner was over. In the living room, Mr. Lambchop looked up from his newspaper. "How nice this is, my dear," he said to Mrs. Lambchop, who was darning socks. "I am enjoying my paper and your company, and our boys are studying in their room."

"Let us hope they are," said Mrs. Lambchop. "So often, George, they find excuses not to work."

Mr. Lambchop chuckled. "They *are* imaginative," he said.

In their bedroom, Stanley and his younger brother, Arthur, *were* doing homework. They wore pajamas, and over his, Arthur also wore his Mighty

Man T-shirt, which helped him to concentrate.

On the desk between them was what they supposed to be a teapot—a round, rather squashed-down pot with a curving spout, and a knob on top for lifting. A wave had rolled it up onto the beach that summer, right to Stanley's feet; and since Mrs. Lambchop was very fond of old furniture and silverware, he had saved it as a gift for her birthday, now only a week away.

The pot was painted dark green, but streaks of brownish metal showed through. To see if polishing would make it shine, Stanley rubbed the knob with his pajama sleeve.

Puff! Black smoke came from the spout.

"Yipe!" said Arthur. "It's going to explode!"

"Teapots don't explode." Stanley rubbed again. "I just—"

Puff! Puff! Puff! They came rapidly now, joining to form a small cloud in the air above the desk.

"Look out!" Arthur shouted. "Double yipes!"

The black cloud swirled, its blackness becoming a mixture of brown and blue, and began to lose its cloud shape. Arms appeared, and legs, and a head.

"Ready or not, here I come!" said a clear young voice.

Now the cloud was completely gone, and a slender, cheerful-looking boy hovered in the air above the desk. He wore a sort of decorated towel on his head, a loose blue shirt, and curious, flapping brown trousers, one leg of which had snagged on the pot's spout.

"Florts!" said the boy, shaking his leg. "Collibots! I got the puffs right, and the scary cloud, but— There!" Unsnagged, he floated down to the

floor and bowed to Stanley and Arthur.

"Who rubbed?" he asked.

Neither of the brothers could speak.

"Well, *someone* did. Genies don't just drop in, you know." The boy bowed again. "How do you do? I am Prince Fawzi Mustafa Aslan Mirza Melek Namerd Haraz. Call me Prince Haraz."

Arthur gasped and dived under his bed.

"What's the matter with him?" the genie asked. "And who are you, and where am I?"

"I'm Stanley Lambchop, and this is the United States of America," Stanley said. "That's Arthur under the bed."

"Not a very friendly welcome," said Prince Haraz. "Especially for someone who's been cooped up in a lamp." He rubbed the back of his neck. "Florts! One thousand years, with my knees right up against my chin. This is my first time out."

"I must have gone crazy," said Arthur from under the bed. "I am just going to lie here until a doctor comes."

"Actually, Prince Haraz, you're here by accident," Stanley said. "I didn't even know that pot was a lamp. Was it the rubbing? Those puffs of smoke, I mean, that turned into you?"

"Were you scared?" The genie laughed. "Just a few puffs, I thought, and I'll *whoooosh* up the spout."

"Scaring *me* wasn't fair," said Arthur, staying under the bed. "I just live in this room because Stanley's my brother. It's his lamp, and he's the

one who rubbed it."

"Then he's the one I grant wishes for," said Prince Haraz. "Too bad for you."

"I don't care," said Arthur, but he did.

"Can I wish for anything?" Stanley asked. "Anything at all?"

"Not if it's cruel or evil, or really nasty," said Prince Haraz. "I'm a lamp genie, you see, and we're the good kind. Not like those big jar genies. They're stinkers."

"Wish for something, Stanley." Arthur sounded suspicious. "Test him out."

"I'll be right back," Stanley said, and went into the living room.

"Hey!" he said to Mr. and Mrs. Lambchop. "Guess what?"

"Hay is for horses, Stanley, not people," Mr. Lambchop said from behind his newspaper. "Try to remember that."

"Excuse me," Stanley said. "But you'll never guess—"

"My guess is that you and Arthur have not yet finished your homework," said Mrs. Lambchop, looking up from her mending.

"We were doing it," said Stanley, talking very fast, "but I have this pot that turned out to be a lamp, and when I rubbed it, smoke came out, and then a genie, and he says I can wish for things, only I thought I should ask you first. Arthur got scared, so he's hiding under the bed."

Mr. Lambchop chuckled. "When your studying is done, my boy," he said. "But no treasure chests full of gold and diamonds, please. Think of the taxes we would pay!"

"There is your answer, Stanley," said Mrs. Lambchop. "Now back to work, please."

"Okay, then," said Stanley, going out.

Mrs. Lambchop laughed. "Treasure

chests, indeed! Taxes! George, you are very amusing."

Behind his newspaper, Mr. Lambchop smiled again. "Thank you, my dear," he said.

The Askit Basket

"I told them, but they didn't believe me," Stanley said, back in the bedroom.

"Of course they didn't." Arthur was still under the bed. "Who'd believe a whole person could puff out of a pot?"

"It's not a *pot*," said Prince Haraz.

"Now please come out. I apologize for the puffs."

Arthur crawled from under the bed. "No more scary stuff?"

"I promise," the genie said, and they shook hands.

Arthur could hardly wait now. "Stanley! Try a wish!"

"We can't," Stanley said. "Not till our homework is done."

"What's homework?" asked Prince Haraz.

The brothers stared at him, amazed, and then Stanley explained. The genie shook his head.

"*After* schooltime, when you could be

having fun?" he said. "Where I come from, we just let Askit Baskets do the work."

"Well, whatever *they* are, I wish I had one," said Stanley, forgetting he was not supposed to wish.

Prince Haraz laughed. "Oh? Look behind you."

Turning, Stanley and Arthur saw a large straw basket, about the size of a beach ball and decorated with red and green zigzag stripes, floating in the air above the desk.

"Yipes!" said Arthur. "More scary stuff!"

"Don't be silly," said the genie. "It's

a perfectly ordinary Askit Basket.
Whatever you want to know, Stanley,
just ask it."

Feeling rather foolish, Stanley leaned forward and spoke to the basket. "I, uh . . . that is . . . uh . . . Can I have the answers for my math homework? It's the problems on page twenty of my book."

The basket made a steady *huuuummmm* sound, and then a man's voice rose from it, deep and rich like a TV announcer's.

"Thank you for calling Askit Basket," it said. "We're sorry, but all our Answer Genies are busy at this time. Your questions will be answered by the first available personnel. While you wait, enjoy a selection by the Genie-ettes."

Stanley stared at the Askit Basket. Music was coming out of it now, the sort of soft, faraway music he had heard in the elevators of big office buildings.

Prince Haraz shrugged. "What can you do? It's a very popular service."

There was a *click* and the music stopped. Now a female voice, full of bouncy good cheer,

came from the basket. "Hi! This is Shireen! Thanks a whole bunch for waiting, and I would like at this time to give you your answers. The first answer is: 5 pears, 6 apples, 8 bananas. The second answer is: Tom is 4 years old, Tim is 7, Ted is 11. The third—"

"Wait!" Stanley shouted. "I can't remember all this!"

"A written record, created especially for your convenience, is in the basket, sir," said the cheery voice. "Thanks for calling Askit Basket, and have a real nice day!"

Lifting the lid of the basket, Stanley saw a sheet of paper with all his answers on it. "Oh, good!" he said. "Thank you. Can my brother talk now, please?"

Arthur cleared his throat. "Hello, Shireen," he said. "This is Arthur Lambchop speaking. For English, I'm supposed to write about 'What I Want to Be.'"

"Certainly, Mr. Lambchop," said the

basket. "Just a teeny moment now, to make sure the handwriting— There! All done!"

Arthur opened the basket and found a sheet of lined paper covered with his own handwriting. He read it aloud.

What I Want to Be
by Arthur Lambchop

When I grow up, I want to be President of the United States so that I can make a law not to have any more wars. And get to meet astronauts. And I would like not to have to go out with girls who want to get all dressed up. Most of all I would like to be the strongest man in the world, like Mighty Man, not to hurt people, but so everybody would be extra nice to me.

The End

Arthur smiled. "That's fine!" he said. "Just what I wanted to say, Shireen."

"Good," said the basket. "'Bye now! Have a super day!"

The brothers called good-bye, and Prince Haraz plucked the basket out of the air and set it on the desk by his lamp.

"There! Homework's done," he said. "That was a very ordinary sort of wish, Stanley. Isn't there anything special you've always wanted? Something exciting?"

Stanley knew right away what he wanted most. He had always loved animals; how exciting it would be to have his own zoo! But that would take up too much space, he thought. Just one animal then, a truly unusual pet. A lion? Yes! What fun it would be to walk down the street with a pet lion on a leash!

"I wish for a lion!" he said. "Real, but friendly."

"Real, but friendly," said the genie. "No problem."

Stanley realized suddenly that a lion would scare people, and that an elephant would be even greater fun.

"An elephant, I mean!" he shouted. "Not a lion. An elephant!"

"What?" said Prince Haraz. "An eleph—? Oh, collibots! Look what you made me do!"

A most unusual head had formed in the air across the room, a head with an elephant's trunk for a nose but with small, neat, lionlike ears. There was a lion's mane behind the head, but then came an elephant's body and legs in a brownish-gold lion color, and finally a little gray elephant tail with a pretty gold ruff at the tip. All together, these parts made an animal about the size of a medium lion or a small elephant.

"My goodness!" said Stanley. "What's that?"

"A Liophant." Prince Haraz seemed annoyed. "It's your fault, not mine.

You overlapped your wish."

The Liophant opened his mouth wide, gave a half roar, half snort *Grrowll-HONK!* that made them all jump, then sat back on his hind legs and went *pant-pant* like a puppy, looking quite nice.

"Well, we got the friendly part right," said the genie. "The young ones mostly are."

Stanley patted him, and Arthur tickled behind the neat little ears. The Liophant licked their hands and Stanley was not at all sorry that he had mixed up his wish.

Just then, a knock sounded on the

bedroom door, and Mrs. Lambchop's voice called out, "Homework done?"

"Come in," said Stanley, not thinking, and the door opened.

"How very quiet you—" Mrs. Lambchop began, and then she stopped. Her eyes moved slowly about the room from Prince Haraz to the Askit Basket, and on to the Liophant.

"Gracious!" she said.

Prince Haraz made a little bow. "How do you do? You are the mother of these fine lads, yes?"

"I am, thank you," said Mrs. Lambchop. "Have we met? I don't seem to—"

"This is Prince Haraz," Stanley said. "And that's a Liophant, and that's an Askit Basket."

"Guess what," said Arthur. "Prince Haraz is a genie, and Stanley can wish for anything he wants."

"How very generous!" Mrs. Lambchop said. "But I'm not sure . . ." Turning, she called into the living room. "George, come here! Something quite unexpected has happened."

"In a moment," Mr. Lambchop called back. "I am reading an unusual story in my newspaper, about a duck who watches TV."

"This is even more unusual than that," she said, and Mr. Lambchop came at once.

"Ah, yes," he said, looking about the room. "Yes, I see. Would someone care to explain?"

"I tried to before," Stanley said. "Remember? About—"

"Wait, dear," said Mrs. Lambchop.

The Liophant had been making snuffling, hungry sounds, so she went off to the kitchen and returned with a large bowl full of hamburger mixed with warm milk. While the Liophant ate, Stanley told Mrs. Lambchop what had happened.

Mr. Lambchop thought for a moment. "Unusual indeed," he said. "And what a fine opportunity for you, Stanley. But I do not approve of using the Askit Basket for your homework, boys. Nor will your teachers, I'm afraid."

"My plan is, let's not tell them," Arthur said.

Mr. Lambchop gave him a long look. "Would you take credit for work you have not done?"

Arthur blushed. "Oh! Well, I guess not . . . I wasn't thinking. Because of all the excitement, you know?"

Mr. Lambchop wrote NOT IN USE on

a piece of cardboard and taped it to the Askit Basket.

"It is too late for more wishing tonight," Mrs. Lambchop said. "Prince Haraz, there is a folding cot in the closet, so you will be comfortable here. Tomorrow is Saturday, which we always spend together in the park. You will join us, yes?"

"Thank you very much," said the genie, and he helped Stanley and Arthur set up the cot.

The Liophant was already asleep, and Mrs. Lambchop picked up his bowl. "Gracious! Three pounds of the best hamburger, and he ate every bit." She put out the light. "Good night to you all."

It was quite dark in the bedroom, but some moonlight shone through the window. From their beds, Stanley and Arthur could see that Prince Haraz was still sitting up in his cot. For a moment all was silence except for the gentle snoring of the Liophant, and then the genie said, "Sorry about the snoring. It's having all that nose, probably."

"It's okay," Arthur said sleepily. "Do genies snore?"

"We don't even sleep," said Prince Haraz. "Your mother was so kind, I didn't want to tell her. She might have felt bad."

"I'll try to stay awake, if you want to talk," Stanley said.

"No thanks," said the genie. "I'll be fine. After all those years alone in the lamp, it's nice just having company."

In the Park

Everyone slept late and enjoyed a large breakfast, particularly the Liophant, who ate two more pounds of hamburger, five bananas, and three loaves of bread.

Then, since all the Lambchops enjoyed tennis, they set out with their rackets for the courts in the big park

close by. Aware that his genie clothes would puzzle people, Prince Haraz borrowed slacks and a shirt from Stanley, and came along.

In the street, they met Ralph Jones, an old college friend of Mr. Lambchop's, whom they had not seen for quite some time.

"Nice running into you, George, and you too, Mrs. Lambchop," said Mr. Jones. "Hello, Arthur. Hello, Stanley. Aren't you the one who was flat? Rounded out nicely, I see."

"You always did have a fine memory, Ralph," Mr. Lambchop said. "Let me introduce our houseguest, Prince

Haraz. He is a foreign student, here to study our ways."

"How do you do?" said the genie. "I am Fawzi Mustafa Aslan Mirza Melek Namerd Haraz."

"How do you do?" Mr. Jones said. "Well, I must be off. Good-bye, Lambchops. Nice to have met you, Prince Fawzi Mustafa Aslan Mirza Melek Namerd Haraz."

"He *does* have a wonderful memory," Mrs. Lambchop said as Mr. Jones walked away.

They set out for the park again.

"How it would surprise Mr. Jones to learn that Prince Haraz is a genie," Mrs. Lambchop remarked. "The whole world would be amazed. Gracious! We'd all be famous, I'm sure."

"I was famous once, when I was flat," Stanley said. "I didn't like it after a while."

"I remember," said Mrs. Lambchop. "Nevertheless, I wish I knew myself what being famous feels like."

Prince Haraz looked at Stanley in a questioning way, and Stanley gave a little nod. The genie smiled and nodded back.

They were just passing the Famous Museum of Art, one of the city's most important buildings. A tour bus, filled with visitors from foreign countries, had stopped before the museum, and a guide was lecturing the passengers through a megaphone.

"Over where those trees are, that's our great City Park!" he announced. "Here, on the right, is the Famous Museum of Art, full of great paintings and statues and— Oh, what a surprise! We're in luck today, folks! That's Mrs. George Lambchop, coming right toward us! Harriet Lambchop herself, in person! Right there, with the tennis racket!"

The tourists cried out in pleased

astonishment, turning in their seats to stare where the guide was pointing.

"What—? He means *you*, Harriet!" said Mr. Lambchop.

"I think so," said Mrs. Lambchop. "Oh, my goodness! They're coming!"

The tourists were rushing from the bus. A Japanese family reached Mrs. Lambchop first, all with cameras.

"Please, Lampchop lady," said the husband, bowing politely. "Honor to take picture, yes?"

"Of course," said Mrs. Lambchop. "I hope you are enjoying our country. But why *my* picture? I'm not—"

"No, no! Famous, famous! Famous Lambchop lady!" cried the Japanese family, taking pictures as fast as they could.

Mrs. Lambchop understood suddenly that her wish had been granted. "Thank you, Prince Haraz!" she said. "What fun!"

She posed graciously for all the tourists and signed dozens of autographs. In the park she was recognized again, and had to do more posing and signing.

It was now midmorning, and all the park's tennis courts were occupied, but the Lambchops' disappointment lessened when they saw a crowd gathered by one court and learned that Tom McRude, the world's best tennis player, was about to lecture and demonstrate his strokes. Tom McRude was known for his terrible temper and bad manners, but the Lambchops were eager to see him nevertheless. With Prince Haraz, they squeezed close to the court, next to the TV-news cameras covering the event.

"None of you can ever be a great tennis player like me," Tom McRude was saying. "But at least you can have the thrill of seeing me."

A little old lady in the crowd gave a tiny sneeze, and he glared at her. "What's the matter with you, granny?"

The old lady burst into tears, and friends led her away.

"What a mean fellow!" Prince Haraz whispered to Stanley.

"I can't stand old sneezing people!" said Tom McRude. "Okay, now I'll show how I hit my great forehand! First—"

"Hold it, Tom!" called the TV-news director. "We've just spotted Harriet Lambchop here. What a break! Maybe she'll say a few words

for our cameras!"

Even Tom McRude was impressed. "*The* Harriet Lambchop? Wow!"

"Swing those cameras this way, fellows!" The director ran over to Mrs. Lambchop, holding out a microphone.

"Wonderful to see you!" he said. "Everybody wants to know your views. Favorite color? What about the foreign situation? Do you sleep in pajamas or a nightgown?"

"Isn't that rather personal?" asked Mr. Lambchop.

"George, please. . . ." Mrs. Lambchop spoke into the microphone. "Thank you all for your kind welcome," she said. "I would just like to say that I'm glad my fans are having such a lovely day in this delightful park."

The crowd cheered and waved, and Mrs. Lambchop waved back and blew kisses. Jealous of the attention she was getting, Tom McRude whacked a tennis ball over the fence behind him.

Noticing, Mrs. Lambchop spoke again into the microphone. "And now, let us give this great champion our attention!"

"Yeah!" growled Tom McRude. When the TV cameras had swung

back to him, he went on. "I need a volunteer, so that I can demonstrate how terrible most players are compared to me!"

Mr. Lambchop thought it would be thrilling to share a court with a champion. Signaling with his racket, he stepped forward.

Tom McRude handed him some balls. "Okay, try a serve."

Mr. Lambchop prepared to serve.

"He's got his feet wrong!" Tom McRude shouted. "And his grip is wrong! Everything is wrong!"

This made Mr. Lambchop so nervous that he served two balls into the net instead of over it.

"Terrible! Terrible! Watch how I do it," said Tom McRude, running to the far side of the court. From there he served five balls, so hard and fast that Mr. Lambchop missed the first four entirely. The fifth one knocked the racket out of his hand.

"Ha, ha!" laughed Tom McRude. "Now let's see you run!"

He began hitting whizzing forehands and backhands at sharp angles across the court, making Mr. Lambchop look foolish as he raced back and forth, getting very red in the face and missing practically every shot.

The other Lambchops grew angry, as did Prince Haraz. "This need not continue, you know," he whispered to Stanley.

Just then, Mr. Lambchop came skidding to a halt before them, banging his knee with his racket as he missed yet another of the champion's powerful shots.

"Ha, ha! This is how *I* give lessons!" shouted Tom McRude.

Mr. Lambchop looked at Stanley, then at Prince Haraz. "Okay," Stanley said, and the genie smiled a little smile.

"Thank you," said Mr. Lambchop. Returning to the court, he called out to the crowd. "Ladies and gentlemen, I will try my serve again!"

Across the net, Tom McRude gave a nasty laugh and slashed his big racket through the air.

Mr. Lambchop served a ball, not into the net this time, but fast as a bullet right where it was supposed to go. Tom McRude's mouth fell open as the ball whizzed past him. "Out!" he shouted. "That ball was out!"

Voices rose from the crowd. "Shame on you!" . . . "The ball was *in*!" . . . "What a liar!" . . . "In, in, in!"

Tom McRude shook his fist. "I'll bet you can't do that again!"

Mr. Lambchop served three more balls, each even faster than the first one, and as perfectly placed. Tom McRude could not even touch them, though the last one bounced up into his nose.

Then Mr. Lambchop rallied with him, gliding swiftly about the court and returning every shot with ease. With powerful forehands, he made Tom McRude run from corner to corner; with little drop shots, he drew the champion up to the net, then lobbed high shots to send him racing back again. Nobody has ever played such great tennis as Mr. Lambchop played that day.

Tom McRude was soon too tired, and too angry, to continue. He threw down his racket and jumped on it.

"You're just lucky!" he yelled. "Besides, I have a cold! And the sun was in my eyes the whole time!" Pushing his way through the crowd, he ran out of the park.

There was tremendous cheering for Mr. Lambchop, who just smiled modestly and waved his racket in a friendly way. Then he came over to where the other Lambchops and Prince

Haraz were standing with the TV-news director.

"You're really *good*," the director said. "Frankly, you looked terrible when you first went out there."

"It takes me a while to get warmed up," Mr. Lambchop said, and led his family away.

Leaving the park, Mrs. Lambchop signed many more autographs, and a reporter from *Famous Faces* magazine was waiting to interview her at home.

"You'll be on the cover of our next issue," said the reporter. "How much do you weigh? Will there be a movie about your life? Who gave you your first kiss?"

"None of your business!" said Mr. Lambchop, and the reporter went away.

They watched the evening news on television, hoping Mr. Lambchop's tennis would be shown, but only Mrs. Lambchop appeared, with Tom McRude in the background. "The celebrated Harriet Lambchop was in the park today," said the newscaster, after which came a close-up of Mrs. Lambchop saying, "I'm glad my fans are having such a lovely day," and that was that.

Dinner was interrupted several times by phone calls for Mrs. Lambchop from newspaper and television people. The calls bothered Mr. Lambchop, but not the Liophant, who ate four pork chops, a jar of peanut butter, a quart of potato salad, and the rubber mat from under his dish.

The Brothers Fly

"I'm not complaining," said Arthur, complaining, "but it's not fair. Some people have Liophants, or get famous. I want to be President, or as strong as Mighty Man, but all I got was one minute with an Askit Basket we can't even use anymore."

It was after dinner, and the brothers

were in their bedroom with Prince Haraz, all in pajamas.

"It's not my fault, Arthur." The genie looked hurt. "I just follow orders. Rub, I appear. Wish, I grant. That's it."

Stanley felt sorry for his brother. "I don't think you should be President, Arthur," he said. "But I'll wish for you to be the strongest man in the world. I wish it, Prince Haraz!"

"Oh, good!" said Arthur.

He waited, but nothing happened. "Darn! It didn't work!" Disappointed, he punched his left hand with his right fist.

"Owwww!" Jumping up and down, Arthur flapped his hand to relieve the pain.

"When you're the strongest man in the world," said Prince Haraz, "you have to be careful what you hit."

"But I still feel like me," Arthur said. Testing himself, he took hold of the big desk with one hand and lifted it easily above his head.

Stanley's mouth flew open, and so did the desk drawers.

Pencils, marbles, and paper clips rained down onto the floor.

"Ooops!" said Arthur.

"This is ridiculous," said Prince

Haraz, helping him tidy up. "The strongest man in the world, in a bedroom picking up desks! Out having adventures, that's where you should be."

"We can't now," Arthur said. "It's almost bedtime."

Stanley had an idea. "There'd be time if we could fly! Can't we all fly somewhere?"

"I've always been able to," said the genie. "For you two, it'll take wishing."

"I wish!" shouted Stanley. "Flying! Arthur and me both!"

For a moment the brothers held

their breath, expecting to be swept up into the air. Then Arthur tried small flapping movements with his elbows.

"Oh, collibots!" said the genie. "Not like that. Just *think* of flying, and where you want to go."

It worked.

Stanley and Arthur found themselves suddenly a few feet off the floor, face down and quite comfortable, and however they wished to go, up or down, forward or back, was how they went. It was like swimming in soft, invisible water, but without the effort of swimming.

Prince Haraz gave advice as the brothers glided happily about the room: "Point your toes. . . . Heads up! . . . Good, very good. . . . Yes, I think you're ready now!"

He opened a window and leaned out. "Hmmm. . . . This breeze may be coolish higher up. We'd better wear something extra."

Stanley and Arthur put on bathrobes and gloves, and the genie chose a red parka and a dragon-face ski mask. Then he said, "Away we go!" and the brothers floated through the window after him, out into the night.

Up! Up! UP! they went, leveling off now and then to practice speeding, but mostly rising steadily higher. Stanley and Arthur flew side by side, gaining confidence from each other, and the genie kept an eye on them from behind.

It was a beautiful night. The sky above them was full of stars. Below them the lights of the city twinkled as brightly as the stars. The brothers' white bathrobes and the genie's red parka shone in the moonlight.

They flew above the big park, where an orchestra was giving a concert. Music floated up to them: the clear, sweet tones of flutes and violins and trumpets; the deep, strong notes of cymbals and drums.

"Oh, I'm enjoying this!" Prince Haraz called through his dragon mask. "So different from inside that lamp!"

The three fliers joined hands and circled the blaze of light from where the orchestra sat. It was like ice-skating to music at a rink, but much more fun.

In the distance, the wing lights of a big airplane blinked across the sky.

"Let's chase it!" Stanley shouted.

Prince Haraz laughed. "Go on! I'll catch up!"

Whoooosh! Whoooosh! Holding their arms by their sides, Stanley and Arthur flashed like rockets across the sky, their bathrobes flapping like the sails of a boat. The big airplane was fast, but the brothers were faster. Catching up, they flew around and around it, looking through the windows at the passengers reading and eating from tiny trays.

Arthur saw a little girl with a comic book. Zooming close to her window, he stretched his neck, trying to read over her shoulder. The little girl looked up and saw him. Being mean, she held the comic book down where

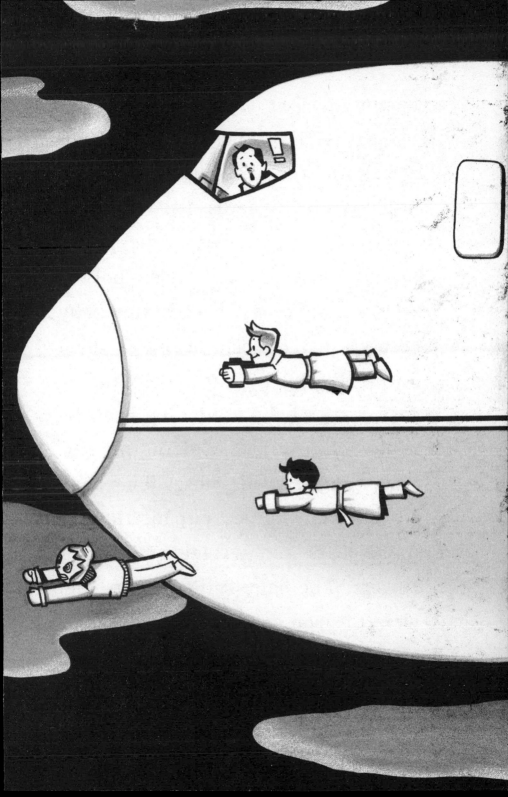

he couldn't see it, and stuck out her tongue. Arthur stuck his tongue out at her, and the little girl scowled and pulled a curtain across her window.

On the other side of the plane, Stanley saw a very tired-looking young couple with a crying baby across their laps, keeping them awake. Flying up next to the window so that the baby could see him, he made a funny face, puffing his lips and wrinkling his nose. The baby smiled, and Stanley put his thumbs in his ears and wriggled his other fingers. The baby smiled again, and went to sleep.

Stanley flew back around the plane, past the cockpit, to join Arthur on the other side.

There were two pilots in the cockpit, and one saw Stanley fly by. Turning his head, he now saw both brothers hovering above a wing tip, waiting for Prince Haraz to catch up.

"Guess what I see out there, Bert," he said.

"The stars in the sky, Tom, and below us the mighty ocean," replied the other pilot.

"No," said Tom. "Two kids in bathrobes."

"Ha, ha! What a joker!" said Bert, but he turned to look.

Only Prince Haraz could be seen now above the wing, his parka flapping as he looked around for Stanley and Arthur, who were hiding from him behind the plane.

"So what do you see, Bert?" asked Tom, keeping his own eyes straight ahead. "Two kids in bathrobes, right?"

"Wrong," said Bert quietly. "I see a guy in ski clothes, with a dragon face."

The pilots stared at each other, then out at the wing again, but the genie had flown to join the brothers behind the plane.

"Nobody there," said Tom. "Let's never mention this to anyone, Bert. Okay?"

"Good idea," said Bert. "Definitely."

They flew on and had nothing more to say.

A giant ocean liner, ablaze with lights, made its way across the sea below.

"Come on!" Arthur shouted, whizzing away with Stanley behind him. Again, Prince Haraz laughed and let them go.

The beauty of the great ship made the brothers marvel as they drew near. It was like an enormous birthday cake, each deck a layer sparkling with the brightness of a thousand candles.

"Look, Stanley!" Arthur cried. "They're having a party on the main deck!"

They flew closer to enjoy the fun and saw then that it was not a party, but a robbery.

The main deck was crowded because robbers had lined up all the passengers and were taking their money and jewelry. The helicopter in which the

robbers had arrived was parked close by, below the captain's bridge. The captain and his fellow officers had struggled, but they were chained up now on the bridge.

"We've got to do something, Stanley!" Arthur said.

Zooming down to the bridge, he shouted over the railing at the robbers below. "Stop, you crooks! Give back all that money and jewelry and stuff!"

Using his great strength, Arthur tore away the ropes and chains that bound the ship's officers. It was as if he were just tearing paper.

Amazed, the robbers stumbled backward, dropping money and jewelry all over the deck.

"Oh, lordy!" one robber yelled. "Who are you?"

Remembering his favorite comic-book hero, Arthur could not resist showing off. He flew ten feet up in the air and stayed there, looking fierce.

"I am Mighty Arthur!" he shouted in a deep voice. "Mighty Arthur, Enemy of Crime!"

Exclamations rose from the robbers and passengers and ship's officers. "So strong, and a flyer too! . . . Who expected Mighty Arthur? . . . Are we ever *lucky*! . . . This ought to be on TV!"

Now Stanley swooped down from the sky with his bathrobe belt untied, so that his robe flared behind him like a cape. "I'm Mighty Stanley!" he called. "Defender of the Innocent!"

"I do that too!" Arthur cried, wishing he had made *his* robe a cape. "We both do good things, but I'm the really strong one!"

He saw suddenly that several robbers were trying to escape in the helicopter. It was already rising, but Arthur flashed through the air until he was directly above it, and with one hand pushed it back down onto the deck. When the frightened robbers jumped out, the ship's officers grabbed them and tied them up.

Now the passengers were even more amazed. "Did you see that?" they said, and "Mighty Arthur and Mighty Stanley, both on the same day!" and "This is *better* than TV!"

The brothers flew up to join Prince Haraz, who had been circling over the ship. "What a pair of show-offs!" said the genie. "Even worse than I used to be."

As they set out for home, the cheers of the grateful passengers and crew floated up behind them. "Hooray for our rescuers!" they heard, and "Especially Mighty Arthur!" and a moment later, "Mighty Stanley too, of course!"

Soon the big ship was no more than an outline of tiny lights in the black sea below, and the last cheer was only a whisper above the rushing of the wind: "Three cheers . . . for . . . the Enemy . . . of . . . Crime . . . and the . . . Defender . . . of the . . . Inno . . . cent!"

The brothers felt very proud, but it had been a tiring adventure, and they were not sorry when the city came into sight.

The Last Wish

Flying back into the bedroom, the three adventurers found Mr. and Mrs. Lambchop waiting anxiously. The Liophant, who had just finished an enormous bowl of spaghetti mixed with chocolate cookies and milk, was asleep.

"Thank goodness!" Mrs. Lambchop ran to hug her sons.

"Where have you been?" Mr. Lambchop was stern. "Is that you, Prince Haraz, behind that dragon face?"

The genie took off his mask. "Were you worried? Sorry. We went for a little flight."

"Wait till you hear!" said Arthur. "You can't tell from looking, but I'm the strongest man in the world, and—"

"Take off those robes and gloves," said Mrs. Lambchop. "It is not wise to get overheated."

She went on, as they put their things away. "*Such* an evening! The phone never stopped. I was asked to go on four TV shows, and to advertise a new soap—they wanted to photograph me in the bathtub, so of course I said no!—and then, to find the window open and the three of you *gone*! Such a fright!"

"We thought we'd be right back," said Stanley, apologizing. "We didn't know so many exciting things would happen."

Everybody sat down, and Stanley told about wishing Arthur strong, and the flying, and chasing the airplane, and the robbers on the ship. Mr. and Mrs. Lambchop both gave deep sighs when Stanley was done.

"It seems, Prince Haraz," Mr. Lambchop said, "that there are often unexpected consequences when wishes come true."

"Oh, yes," said the genie. "That's what got me into a lamp."

"It's not just the Askit Basket problem," Mr. Lambchop said. "Mrs. Lambchop has been famous less than a day, and already she is exhausted and has lost all her privacy. And though Tom McRude deserved what he got, his tennis comes from natural

ability. I am not proud of having shamed him by using magic."

"And Arthur's great strength will make other boys afraid of him," Mrs. Lambchop said. "And flying, mixing with criminals . . . Dear me! We must consider all this. I will make hot chocolate. It is helpful when there is serious thinking to be done."

Everyone enjoyed the delicious hot chocolate she brought from the kitchen, with a marshmallow for each cup. The Lambchops sat quietly, sipping and thinking. Prince Haraz, having said twice that he was sorry to have caused problems, began to pace up and down. The Liophant was still asleep.

At last Mr. Lambchop put down his cup and cleared his throat. "Your attention, please," he said, and they all looked at him.

"Here is my opinion," he said. "Genies and their magic, Prince Haraz, are fine for faraway lands and long-ago times, but the Lambchops have always been quite natural people, and this is the United States of America, and the time is today. We are grateful for the excitement you have offered, but now I must ask: Is it possible for Stanley to *un*wish all the wishes he has made?"

"It is, actually," said the genie.

"How clever of you, George!" cried Mrs. Lambchop.

Arthur sighed. "I don't know. . . . I really like the flying. But being so strong, I guess nobody *would* play with me."

"I care most about the Liophant," Stanley said. "Couldn't we just keep him?"

"He is very lovable," said Mrs. Lambchop. "But he never stops eating! We cannot *afford* to keep him."

"Sad, but true," Mr. Lambchop said.

"Now please tell us, Prince Haraz, what must be done."

"It's called Reverse Wishing." The genie took the little green lamp from the desk and turned it over. "The instructions should be right here on the bottom. Let's see. . . ."

He studied the words carved into the bottom of the lamp. "Seems simple enough. Each wish has to be separately reversed. I just say 'Mandrono!' and—" His voice rose. "Oh, collibots! Double florts! See that little circle there? This is a *training* lamp! There may not be enough wishes left!"

"A training lamp?" exclaimed Mr.

Lambchop. "What is that?"

"They're for beginners like me, so we don't overdo for one person," Prince Haraz said unhappily. "The little 'fifteen' in the circle, that's all the wishes I'm allowed for Stanley."

The Lambchops all spoke at once. "What? . . . You never told us! . . . Only fifteen? . . . Oh, dear!"

"Please, I'm embarrassed enough," said the genie, very red in the face. "A *training* lamp! As if I were a baby!"

"We are all beginners, at one time or another," said Mr. Lambchop. "What matters is, are fifteen wishes enough?"

The genie counted on his fingers to be sure he got it right. "Askit Basket, Liophant—lucky he doesn't count double!—that's two, and fame for Mrs. Lambchop and the fancy tennis, that's four. Making Arthur strong is five, flying for him *and* Stanley is two more . . ." He smiled. "Seven, and seven for reversing is fourteen! One wish left over for some sort of good-bye treat!"

"Thank goodness!" Mrs. Lambchop hesitated. "It is very late. Could you begin the reversing *now*, do you think?"

Prince Haraz nodded. "I'll do the

whole family in a bunch. Let's see . . .
Strength, famous, tennis, two flying.
Ready, Arthur? No more Mighty Man
after this, I'm afraid."

"Will I feel weak?" Arthur asked.
"Will I flop over?"

The genie shook his head.
"Mandrono!" he said. "Mandrono,
Mandrono, Mandrono, Mandrono!"

Arthur felt a prickling on the back of
his neck. When the prickling stopped,
he gave the big desk a shove, but couldn't
budge it.

"I'm just regular me again," he said.
"Oh, well."

"And I am just Harriet Lambchop

again," said Mrs. Lambchop, smiling. "An unimportant person."

"To all of us, my dear, you are the most important person we know," said Mr. Lambchop. "Arthur, you are as strong as you were yesterday. Think of it that way."

The genie sipped the last of his hot chocolate. "Where was I? Oh, yes . . ." He glanced at the Askit Basket. "Mandrono!" The basket vanished. "Just the Liophant now," he said.

Everyone looked at the Liophant, who was sitting up now in the corner, scratching behind his lion ears with

his elephant trunk. Stanley patted
him, and the Liophant licked his
hand.

"How sweet!" Mrs. Lambchop said.
"George, perhaps. . . ?"

"What makes Liophants truly
happy," said the genie, "is open
spaces, and the company of other
Liophants."

"Then send him
where it's like
that," Stanley
said bravely,

patting again. The Liophant vanished halfway through the pat.

For a moment no one spoke.

"Good for you, Stanley," Mr. Lambchop said softly. "And now you must think of a last wish to make."

While Stanley thought, Mrs. Lambchop collected the hot chocolate cups. "Where will you go now, Prince Haraz?" she said.

"Back into that stuffy little lamp," said the genie. "And then it's wait, wait, wait! Hundreds and hundreds of years, probably. It's my punishment for playing too many tricks. My friends warned me, but I wouldn't listen."

He sighed. "Mosef, Ali, Ben Sifa, little Fawz. Such wonderful fellows! I think of them when I'm alone in the lamp, the *fun* they must be having. The games, the freedom. . . ." His voice trembled, and the Lambchops felt very sorry for him.

Suddenly, Arthur had an idea. He whispered it to Stanley.

"Why the whispering?" the genie said crossly. "Let's have that last wish, Stanley, and I'll smoke back into my lamp."

The brothers were smiling at each other. "Good idea, right?" said Arthur.

"Oh, yes!" Stanley turned to the genie. "Here is my last wish, Prince Haraz. I wish for you *not* to stay in the lamp, but to go back where you came from, to be with your genie friends and have good times with them, forever from now on!"

Prince Haraz gasped. His mouth fell open.

Mr. Lambchop worried that he might faint. "Are you all right?" he asked. "Is Stanley not allowed to set you free?"

"Yes, yes . . . it's allowed." The genie spoke softly. "But nobody ever used a wish for the sake of a genie.

Not until now."

"How selfish people can be!" said Mrs. Lambchop.

Prince Haraz rubbed his eyes. "What a fine family this is," he said, beginning to smile. "I thank you all. The name of Lambchop will be honored always, wherever genies meet."

His smile enormous now, he shook hands with each of the Lambchops. The last shake was with Stanley, and the genie was already a bit smoky about the edges. By the time he let go of Stanley's hand, he was all smoke, a dark cloud that swirled briefly over the little lamp

on the desk, then poured in through the spout until not a puff remained.

Full of wonder, the Lambchops gathered about the lamp, and after a moment Arthur put his lips to the spout.

"Good-bye, Prince Haraz!" he called. "Have a nice trip!"

From within the lamp, a faraway voice called back, "Bless you all. . . ." And then there was only silence in the room.

Mr. Lambchop was the first to speak. "I'm proud of you, Stanley," he said. "Your last wish was generous and kind."

"It was my idea, actually," Arthur

said, and Mrs. Lambchop kissed the top of his head. "Off to bed now, boys," she said. "Tomorrow is another day."

Stanley and Arthur got into bed, and she turned out the light.

"The lamp was supposed to be a surprise birthday present," Stanley said sleepily. "Now it won't be a surprise at all."

"I will love it anyhow," said Mrs. Lambchop. "And Prince Haraz was a tremendous surprise. Good night, my dears."

She kissed them both, and so did Mr. Lambchop, and they went out.

The brothers lay quietly in the

darkness for a while, and then Stanley sighed. "I miss the Liophant a bit," he said. "But I don't mind about the rest."

"Me neither." Arthur yawned. "Florts, Stanley, and good night."

"Good night," Stanley said. "Collibots."

"Mandrono," murmured Arthur, and soon they were both asleep.

The End

JEFF BROWN created the beloved character of Flat Stanley as a bedtime story for his sons. He wrote six books about the Lambchop family's madcap adventures.

MACKY PAMINTUAN is an accomplished illustrator who's brought a special look to all the books in the Flat Stanley series. He lives in the Philippines with his wife, daughter, and dog.